The War
of the
Dead

LATILYA SIVAR

ISBN: 978-1478289647

In memory of Volrin Dahl. Author, truth seeker, and friend.

CONTENTS

The
Necromancer's
Bargain

LATILYA
SIVAR

Any resident of Midgar could tell you the story of the War of the Dead. The tale of the vile necromancer that came out of the forsaken forest, and with his wicked sorcery, created an army of the dead to destroy the world of men. The few survivors of the onslaught fled to Midgar, where they held off the armies of the dead for years, until at long last the necromancer gave up, and returned to the northlands with his unliving army. They would go on to say that the necromancer to this day sits upon his throne of skulls, plotting the final destruction of humanity. It is a story of ancient villains, and young heros, and the story defines Midgar's character as a nation.

Unfortunately few first hand accounts remain from the time of the war, and those that do exist contradict each other. Recently, however, when sorting through my family's old records, I found a collection of accounts written by my ancestor, who worked as a spy during the conflict. The following is what I believe to be the true story of the time leading up to the War of the

Dead, and the implications are staggering.

Our story begins with a woodcutter named Drel. He lived in the lumber village of Thorlin's Point, within what we have now come to call the forsaken forest. At the time it was simply the forest, as there were no other forests within the domain of humanity. The one oddity of living in the forest was that funerals were not done. When a man or woman died their body would disappear on the same night. Nobody thought particularly much of this, as most who lived in the forest were born and raised there. It was simply an unexplained oddity.

Recently the people of Thorlin's Point had come upon hard times, as their lords in Thelryn had stopped purchasing their lumber. Tempers were flaring, and the villagers were worried about their ability to survive another year.

Amidst the turmoil caused by the situation with Thelryn Drel began to have nightmares. He would wake in the dead of night drenched with sweat and feeling violated, as if someone had been looking through his very soul. Sometimes he felt a presence in his room when he awoke, others he felt profoundly alone, as if he were the only person left in a world of terrors. He tried to shrug off the nightmares, attributing them to stress. He took naps in the afternoons to make up for his lack of sleep at night, and stayed out later at the bar to avoid going home. With the lack of work lately, the nightmares had proven to be only a minor nuisance.

On a night like any other, Drel was drinking with a friend at the bar and listening to him rant about Thelryn for the third time this week, not suspecting that his entire world was about to change.

"I'm tellin' ya Drel it just ain't right! We got all this lumber sittin' in storage an' nothin' to do with it! Them city dwellers don't give a damn about our issues!"

Drel nodded absent mindedly, having heard it all before. "They've never cared about us, Corin, we've been fine so-"

Corin pounded a hand on the table. "Fine?! You know as well as I do we're runnin' low on supplies! If we don't sell that lumber we'll be out of basic necessities within a month!"

Drel shook his head. "Calm down Corin, beer doesn't count as a basic necessity. We have time to come up with a solution."

Corin scowled. "Didn't you tell me a few weeks ago you're down to your last sheepskin? The ladies aren't going to be happy if you run out."

Drel laughed. "I think they'll survive Corin. I've been sleeping alone lately regardless. I recently learned that when awoken by a beautiful woman, a scream of terror is not an appropriate greeting for her. It took weeks for Pelre to forgive me for that particular slight." Drel took on a look of the purest remorse. "These nightmares are truly horrible Corin, not for the pain they cause me, but for their effects on those I hold dear."

Corin first looked bewildered, and then burst out into a riotous laugh. "So that's how your nightmares became common knowledge. I'd heard you and her had a falling out but I didn't get the details."

Drel managed to hold his remorseful expression for a few moments, before laughing himself. "We all make sacrifices in these dark times my friend. We'll get through this, and soon you'll have all the beer you can drink, and I can stop neglecting my duties as an eligible bachelor."

Corin sighed heavily. "That's true I suppose, but it's never been this bad before, Drel. If Thelcrest keeps up the pace they're setting, Thelryn is going to let this town die entirely."

Drel sighed and leaned back in his chair to stare at the ceiling. The barkeepers pet crow was sitting in the rafters watching them, probably waiting for them to leave so it could help itself to the scraps from their dinner. After a few moments watching the bird, he sighed again, and looked back to Corin.

"I know we're in a tight spot right now Corin, but there's not much we can do about it. If we try to sell to Ilar, we'll just end up starting a war with us in the middle. We've sent some people to Thelcrest to hopefully set up a deal until Thelryn comes to their senses, and we'll just have to hope that goes well for now."

Corin scowled into his ale. "I don't see how you stay so calm about this stuff."

Drel chuckled and stood up. "I just try not to get worked up about things I can't change. If we can't work out a deal with Thelcrest, we'll figure out something else. Anyway, I'm going to bed Corin, you should do the same. We have another big day of not cutting down trees tomorrow."

Corin snorted. "Of course. I can't wait."

After ensuring his intoxicated friend was heading the right direction, Drel headed for his own home. As he walked through the dark streets, he occasionally caught sight of fluttering shapes flying from roof to roof and wondered just how late it was. If the birds were waking up it must be near morning, though it seemed too dark to be close to dawn.

He arrived at home without incident, trying not to think about the dreams he would be having this night. He went through his nightly rituals, locking the door to his bedroom and latching his window shut. It never seemed to help with the nightmares, but it gave him some small sense of security regardless. Feeling bolstered by his rituals, he fell immediately to sleep.

**

'It's not like you to be so hasty Comanatin, weren't you going to expand your influence slowly?'

'There's been a change of plans.'

'I see. Do you really want to start a war? The last time we fought for humans they turned on us. Do you really want to go through that again?'

'It will be different this time, Gingko.'

'Do you think your little pet project will really make such a difference? You can't change human nature.'

'I'll keep things under control, don't worry.'

'I'm not worried you old fool. I'm not the one that made the mistake of planting myself within their reach.'

'I'll be fine, the only risk here is Sveria. She's still alive.'

'Sveria? Are you insane? You're going to start a war with the Bloodletter in the area?'

'She has gone soft from centuries with no real competition. She's still dangerous, but she's no longer the juggernaut she once was. So long as I choose the field she won't be an issue.'

'You can't choose the field if she decides to massacre a city that you don't happen to be in, Comanatin. Soft or not there's no way the humans can survive a war with her, and if you come across

her mid-massacre she'll kill you. What are you thinking? Is this some scheme of yours to get me involved?'

'Nothing like that, Gingko. I have a plan to deal with her on my own. It won't be easy, but the situation is never going to improve. I have eyes everywhere now. She can't move without me knowing about it. I'll keep her contained, and away from my living forces.'

'You really think that's possible? I think you're underestimating her, Comanatin.'

'We shall see. You have permission to admonish me should I turn out to be wrong'

'I'll be sure to take you up on that. I know better than to try to reason with you about things like this.'

'Yes. I think we've both learned that argument about such matters is pointless, though I do appreciate your input. Enough about my plans though. How is your little dragon war going?'

'The dragons are as bad as the humans. They just don't give up. The only reason I haven't moved is because they have such useful parts. I created new bodies for Wraith and Shade entirely out of dragons.'

'Are they still attacking you?'

'No, I have a bit of a reprieve for now since I killed the one that was inspiring the attacks. It's remarkable to me that they attack because I use pieces of their dead, and yet they never realize that if not for them assaulting me I wouldn't have any parts for them to be angry about.'

'Dragons were never known for their sense, Gingko. They're too aggressive for their own good.'

'The same can be said of humans, old friend.'

'I'll keep that in mind. Don't worry Gingko. If this falls apart I'll get out safely, and I'm sure you'll be waiting to say "I told you so".'

'I'll hold you to that promise, Comanatin.'

**

Drel snapped awake upon feeling a sense of intrusion. His room was silent and dark, lit only by the moonlight that streamed through the open window. It didn't look damaged, and he was sure he would have heard it if someone had forced it open from the outside, but it was quite clearly open now regardless. The sense of intrusion he felt seemed to come from the darkness outside the window, but before he could think on it further a sharp pain distracted him, and out of reflex he brought his hand down upon his thigh, crushing the spider that had bitten his leg.

Distracted from the window, he finally noticed what he at first thought was the walls moving. Despite the darkness that engulfed the room, he could barely make out an amorphous mass covering the walls, that seemed to be leaking down to the floor. As the mass reached the floor, it began moving toward his bed, and, reaching the light streaming through the window, revealed itself to be a swarm of insects.

Putting off the question of "why?" for later, he looked around the room for a means of escape. The door was still locked, but going through the window would be simple enough. He'd gone through his share of ladies' windows while their parents were knocking on the door to be let in and he was well able to do it in a rush. As the edge of the swarm was climbing up the sides of his bed he made his decision and sprung off the bed toward the window, crushing some of the bugs with his bare feet and being bit by others in the split second before he ran two more steps and leapt toward the open window, grabbing the sill with his hands and pulling himself up only to smash his head into what distinctly felt like closed shutters.

Stunned by the impact, he fell and landed on the swarm with the crunch of cracking exoskeletons. He blinked and was suddenly in total darkness, his shutters closed and latched as he'd left them when he fell asleep. He felt the swarm engulf him and begin biting his hands, feet, and head. He leapt to his feet, desperately trying to unlatch the window, but it wouldn't move, as if the latch had fused together. More were biting him now, some climbing up his legs and arms, while others dropped from the ceiling to land on him. The pain was excruciating now, the mixture of poisonous stings and ripping mandibles worse than either would be alone. He ran to his door, fumbling with the latch as the tiny creatures continued tearing into his flesh. He tried slamming into the door but all he accomplished was smashing some of the bugs on his shoulder and knocking even more onto him from the door. He tried once more, the pain reaching unbearable levels, before returning to the window and slamming into it with his shoulder, trying to break it out. The window didn't even shudder. It felt like ramming into a stone wall. Finally, his frustration and agony peaking, he screamed "Just leave me alone!" before collapsing into welcome darkness.

**

Drel awoke on his bed with a start. The pain was gone and his room was unchanged from when he had fallen asleep the night before. Trace amounts of light were streaming in through the cracks in the closed window shutters, and there was no sign of any intrusion. He stood up quickly, and looking down on himself, saw no sign of the stings he clearly remembered from the night. His confusion gave way to more reasoned thought as his mind awoke fully, and the last vestiges of sleep left him. Clearly it had just been another nightmare, though he wondered why this was the first he could remember. Shaking off the lingering feeling of violation, he opened his window to the welcome sun, and after taking a deep breath of the morning air, prepared himself for another day.

With the storage full, and no buyers on the horizon, Drel was without a job. He decided to go for a walk in the forest to pass some time, not wanting to go to the tavern so early in the day. As he walked the familiar paths, he put his worries behind him, and simply enjoyed the beauty of the forest around him.

After a time, his wanderings brought him to the lumber camp. It hadn't been in use in over a month, and it seemed wrong for a place that usually had so many boisterous workers to be so empty. As if in answer to this thought, a loud cawing sound spread through the area, and looking to the top of the storage building, he saw a large crow looking at him.

Drel laughed at this. "My dearest pardons, sir. I see you've been looking after the place!".

Drel stopped laughing as he heard a howl to the north. Wolves were reasonably common in the area, and they avoided humans for the most part, but it would be foolhardy to stay out this deep in the forest alone with predators around. After giving the crow an exaggerated bow in farewell, he chuckled to himself and turned back down the path south toward the village.

He set a brisk pace. He didn't want the wolves to stumble across him if they happened to be heading the same direction, though he doubted they would be heading closer to the village. He was making good time, though the familiar path was taking some unexpected turns. He was finding himself oddly confused, had he managed to forget the lay of this path in only a month, after years of taking it every day? Another howl sounded, and this time it seemed much closer. More than a little alarmed, but certain he was getting close to the village, he picked up the pace only to find a few moments later, that he was back where he started. He had somehow ended up on the north side of the lumber camp.

The crow was still sitting atop the storage shed, and as he stepped into the clearing, it cawed again, cocking its head to watch him with one black eye. Drel was reminded that crows are scavengers, and the thought of this creature taking such an interest in him with wolves in the area seemed strangely foreboding. He looked away from the bird, and shaking the thought from his head, began walking back to the south end of the camp. More howls erupted from the north, and it was clear they were heading this direction. This reminded him that there was no path on the north side of the camp, and turning back in that direction, he found the path that had dropped him off at the camp was nowhere to be seen.

Drel was truly worried now, and he set off along the southern path again, this time keeping an eye on the sun through the trees to keep his bearings. He quickly came across an unfamiliar turn in the path leading north, and rather than trust the path, he instead headed southwest into the forest. Using the sun as his guide, he moved quickly through the forest, though the howls seemed closer each passing second.

After a short time, he found the trees thinning, and inexplicably, saw the lumber camp again. The crow was still seated in the same perch, and was looking straight at him. Suddenly the howls rang out again, this time seeming to come from all directions, and very close by.

Drel made a snap decision, and ran for the storage building. The howls were behind him now, and as he arrived at the building he threw aside the latch, and ducked inside. He looked out and caught a glimpse of bear sized lupine shapes moving in the trees. Shuddering at the thought that a wolf that size must be some sort of monster, Drel closed the door behind him and looked around for something to bar it with. As his eyes adjusted to the dark of the shed he noticed movement from among the piles of logs, and massive lupine shadows began to coalesce in his vision. With a shout of terror he threw the door back open, and was immediately thrown to the ground outside as an enormous wolf pounced on him from behind.

Drel tried to stand back up, but the creature held him pinned to the ground, and looking up, he saw the rest of the pack approaching from all directions. The wolves were simply massive, at least twice the size of any wolf he'd ever seen. The crow cawed again from its perch on the building, and the wolves all looked at it curiously, as if waiting for something. After another caw, Drel heard the flapping of wings as the crow flew off toward the north.

As the crow flew off, the weight on his back lifted,

and he jumped to his feet, thinking to use the opportunity to escape. He hadn't gotten more than two steps before the wolves tightened their circle, snapping at him as he came across their wall of flesh, fur, and teeth. He stood perfectly still, trying to figure out a way out of this mess, and confused by the strange behavior of the wolves.

The wolf that had pounced on him before snorted, and as Drel turned to look at it, cocked its head to the north and began walking in that direction. The other wolves seemed to take this as a signal, and the tight circle dissolved into a semicircle, leaving the way north clear. One of the wolves nudged Drel from behind with its head, and seeing no way but forward, he followed the pouncer as it led him north into the forest.

Drel fretted as the wolves led him through the forest. The camp was relatively close to the mountains on the north side, and these monstrous wolves were bringing to mind the stories of the creatures that lived in those mountains.

Looking to the wolves, he saw that while their enormous size lent them a far more menacing appearance than their smaller cousins, they also seemed more clean and frankly beautiful than other wolves. Their coats seemed well maintained, and they lacked the scars and bald patches that plagued most wolves he had seen. He laughed to himself.

"Well at least I'm being lead to certain death by the wolven nobility! I wouldn't want to be murdered by a bunch of commoners!"

He heard a bizarre sound from the wolves, a sort of rhythmic panting, and he got the sudden impression he was being laughed at.

"I guess it wouldn't surprise me if these monsters could understand me. It's not like my day hasn't been strange enough already."

The wolf leading him snorted again, gave him a menacing look, and then turned away again

"Oh excuse me, by monsters I, of course, meant beautiful creatures of grace and glory."

The panting laughter started again, and Drel became convinced these things really could understand him.

"If it's all the same to you, would you mind letting me go? I'm really not fond of being devoured."

The wolf ahead shook its head, but otherwise ignored the request.

Drel thought for a moment, and thinking he might as well ask the obvious question, he did so. "Are you going to kill me?"

The wolf shook its head again.

Drel nodded. The wolf could be lying of course, but they hadn't been particularly rough with him earlier. He felt more comfortable knowing that communication was at least possible. He always felt that any problem could be worked out by talking it out.

They continued in silence for a time, until Drel noticed a stone tower ahead of them through the trees. It was quite tall, and Drel was shocked to see it, as it should have been clearly visible even from the village at that height, yet Drel had never seen it before.

"Is that where we're going?"

The wolf nodded its head, and picked up the pace. As they arrived at the tower, Drel noticed there were no windows. It seemed well-maintained, more well-maintained than his own home for that matter. The stone was polished, and the wooden door was spotless. The wolves led him to the door, and the pouncer sat beside it, giving the impression for a moment of a pet dog rather than the enormous wolf that it was. Drel walked up to the door, and noticing there was no knocker, knocked with his hand instead.

The wolf shook its head, and standing up, pushed the door open with its paw. A voice came from inside.

"Come in, Drel. I would have thought sending my familiars to collect you would have been invitation enough."

Drel pushed the door open the rest of the way, and entered the dimly lit tower. There was an enormous staircase snaking its way to the top of the tower, and several doors leading to other rooms on this floor. It was difficult to make out details because of the dim lighting, which seemed to come from everywhere and nowhere at the same time. In the center of the room was a man in dark robes, standing in front of a large table.

"Welcome to my home, Drel. Is the lighting acceptable? I long since have learned to do without, and I can't recall how much is truly necessary."

Drel shook his head, bewildered by the odd statement. "It's pretty dark, sir."

The light level in the room suddenly changed, and it was as bright as day, though the source of the light still remained unclear. Drel could see now that the tower was quite simple. Every surface was extremely clean, but there was no ornamentation whatsoever. The only objects in the room were the table and a large container sitting beside it, and of course, the figure that stood waiting for him to take in his surroundings.

After a short pause Drel spoke. "So why did you send your wolves to chase me down? Wouldn't it have been simpler to come get me yourself?"

The figure paused a moment before answering. "An odd question. Most would ask why I wanted to see them to begin with."

Drel shrugged. "I figure that question will be answered inevitably anyway, I'm more curious about the bizarre summons."

The figure nodded. "Well-reasoned. I sent my wolf familiars because I needed one final test before I felt comfortable meeting you. I wouldn't have survived as long as I have without being careful."

Drel thought on this. "Are the dreams I've been having related to these tests? And the bizarre experience I had with the forest paths?"

The figure's tone became somewhat sad. "I have to apologize for the dreams as you call them. The reason you couldn't remember them is because there were in fact, no dreams. The feelings you experienced upon waking was your will reacting to my investigations. I know they were unpleasant, but they were unfortunately necessary before I met you."

Drel shook his head. "I remembered last night's dream with the bugs."

"Another test I'm afraid. I didn't want to risk you influencing my familiars without seeing you in action during a stressful situation at least once. The bugs were very real, and largely unaffected by your abilities."

Drel frowned. "I take it all these tests of yours are related to some sort of ability you think I have? I'm a pretty normal guy."

The figure laughed. "How many people do you know who have no enemies, Drel? How many men have gone through their lives without ever being in a situation they couldn't talk themselves out of?"

Drel opened his mouth to answer, then went silent and thought about it. "I'll admit I'm pretty good with people. You seem to think that's very dangerous. Are you worried I'll convince you to decorate this place or something?"

The figure chuckled. "Nothing like that I'm afraid. You see your will travels through your words, and influences those around you. Your ability with people goes beyond mere charisma or wit, and I needed to learn more about it."

"My will? Are you talking about mind control? I'm not a demon."

The figure shook his head. "No, not mind control, but definitely influence. Your will enhances your every word, subtly invading the listeners thoughts, and making them more amiable toward you. It is a somewhat unique gift, as manipulating another's mind at all is very difficult, but it turns out your gift is not particularly strong at the moment."

Drel shook his head. "I didn't understand all of that, but I don't try to manipulate others."

"You don't need to try in order to succeed, Drel. You try to reason with people, you try to calm people, and on occasion, you try to incite people. All of these things are manipulation on some level, and you are especially good at it."

Drel tried to take this in, and understand where

this person was coming from. He clearly wanted something or he wouldn't have brought Drel here, and that something likely related to Drel's people skills, though he didn't trust the gibberish the man spouted about the details of that. He decided he would need to learn more about this man before he could make any solid conclusions.

"So who are you?"

"I am Comanatin. I live in this tower, and do my research in solitude. Or I did until recently."

"What changed recently?" Drel asked.

"I finally finished my research on restoring and regenerating the mind."

Drel thought a moment before responding. "You just mentioned that minds are very difficult to work with."

'But not impossible.'

Drel nearly jumped out of his skin, startled by the voice suddenly speaking directly into his mind.

'As I said, you have a remarkably unique talent, but you aren't particularly powerful yet. I have an offer for you, and I want you to give it serious consideration before you respond.'

Drel shook his head, recovering from the bizarre sensation of having another person speak into his mind "What's your offer?"

'I have eyes' Drel immediately thought of the crows. *'yes, my other familiars, in the citystates of Ilar and Thelryn. The nobility in both cities are playing the peasants for fools. The hatred Ilar and Thelryn have for each other does not extend to the nobility, who work together to keep the status quo in place. Thelcrest has recovered from the disaster that resulted in the creation of Thorlin's Point nearly two hundred years ago, and the nobles have decided that Thelryn's ownership of Thorlin's Point has become unbalancing. Ilar is sending forces to destroy the village, and Thelryn is going to allow*

the attack on their territory, while shifting the blame to bandits to prevent demand for a war. It has already been decided.'

Drel cried out, "That's impossible! Why would Thelryn work with Ilar?"

'Think on this and you'll have your answer. Who do you share more in common with? Lady Cruor of Thelryn, or the woodcutter Cerin of Ilcrest?'

Drel shuddered. "Why should I trust you? You're a hermit in a tower with extremely large wolves."

'I see no reason for you to trust me. Ilar will strike within days. Time has run out. Your people have no chance of fending them off on their own, but I can help. I offer you the power to defend your people, as well as yourself. I am offering you revolution.'

Drel glanced around warily. "What kind of power are you talking about? Your wolves are certainly strong, but surely you're not suggesting sending them against trained soldiers?"

'Oh they will have their uses, but that is not what I refer to. One moment while I invite someone to join us.'

Moments later the front door opened and a familiar looking young man, walked in, and seeing Drel, smiled.

"Hey Drel, long time no see."

Drel wracked his brain, trying to think of who this could be. "Do I know you?"

The man laughed. "I should hope so, I was your boss for ten years. Don't tell me you've forgotten?"

Drel shook his head. The man before him clearly looked like Ulter, but Ulter was dead, and he had been almost fifty when he died; this man was clearly no older than twenty-five.

"Do I look that different? I suppose you knew me

toward the end of my first life."

Drel rounded on Comanatin. "So this is where the bodies go when people die? You take them?"

Comanatin said nothing, but Ulter was clearly annoyed at being ignored. "I see how it is, I die a little and you think that means you can just ignore me? I'm still your superior, young man!"

Ulter laughed and continued more cheerfully. "Comanatin saved my life. I'm now stronger, healthier, and happier than ever. Don't you dare complain about him saving me!"

Drel sat on the floor, this was just too much to take in. "So you were dead, but now you're alive again?"

Ulter laughed. "Better than ever, Drel. Comanatin's really onto something. You wouldn't believe how strong I am now. Listen, I know this is alot to take in all at once, but here's the scoop. Comanatin has only worked with the dead up until now, but he can improve the living too. You can be stronger, faster, and recover from any wound. It's great."

Drel nodded absently. "And the catch?"

Ulter shrugged. "No catch."

Drel pondered this, then turned to Comanatin. "And what about your protection? Surely you aren't going to suggest that you thought someone being a people person was a threat, but a bunch of super humans aren't."

Comanatin nodded. "I've taken...precautions."

Drel thought some more. "You've probably altered their minds somehow. Is that what you were doing to me that caused the dreams?"

'No, altering the mind of the unwilling is near impossible. I was merely taking a look, trying to guess at the structure of your will.

19

If I had tried to make any changes…your will would have lashed out dangerously, and you might never have woken up. As an animal becomes self destructive when stressed, so too does the will.'

Drel was shaking his head. "No. You just said that I alter people's minds with my speech, you're contradicting yourself."

'Your will is rather remarkably subtle. You are a charismatic and attractive person, and because of that, people are prone to like you. Your will simply feeds off of the positive feelings that people already have for you, and expands those feelings to touch other areas. The target is, in a sense, a willing participant.'

Drel stood back up. "You have an answer for everything, don't you?"

Comanatin shook his head almost sadly. "Not yet."

Drel thought a few more moments. "You never answered my question earlier. Did you alter the minds of Ulter and the wolves? The dead can't be unwilling can they?"

'I have made a few minor adjustments to protect myself, and if you wish to consider that the catch, there it is. If you accept my gift you will never be able to raise your hand against me, nor actively work to cause me harm.'

Drel considered this. "And how do I know that's the extent of the changes?"

"Frankly you do not. I think you realize that nothing I can say will prove that point. I will tell you this. My goal is to grant the world immortality. Death is a disease that I fully intend to abolish from this planet, and you can help me with that. I am not a charismatic man, and your skills would greatly help my cause. You will have a position of responsibility, but in return for that service you will gain immortality, as well as the liberation of your people."

Drel shook his head. "Why do you care? If you can just restore the dead, does it even matter if I say yes or no? If we all die, won't you just reanimate us anyway?"

'It's not that simple, Drel. Reanimating the dead takes time and energy, all the while corpses decay. If I allow you all to die when Ilar arrives I won't be able to restore the entire village, or even most of it. A few of the villagers will be fine, and the others will be stuck with various states of mental decay. Memories, personalities, all these things are far too complicated to reconstruct fully from a decayed mind.'

Drel contemplated this for a moment. "If that's the case, wouldn't you help regardless of any decision of mine? If you were so benevolent wouldn't you save the village without my involvement?"

'If I were to save the village, it would begin a war. Your village has no means of supporting itself. If I were to protect Thorlin's Point from the wayfarers, what change is being made fundamentally? The village cannot sustain itself for long, you are a specialized economy. Am I to invade your enemies as a tyrant? No. I have no interest in such things. The only path for your people is the path of independence. I will aid no doomed cause.'

Drel thought on this before responding. "And what does that have to do with me? I don't speak for the entire village."

'You do, in fact. The discontent is already there. All you need do is rally the people. They feel powerless, held down by a group that is untouchable. You simply need to give them the power to stand.'

Drel thought on all this. If what this necromancer said was true his village was doomed without aid. Even if they managed to survive the initial assault, Ilar would just send more troops. His village had defended itself from the occasional monster that wandered in out of the mountains, but he didn't like their odds against a citystate. If the necromancer was lying...did it really matter? If he could raise the dead and tame monstrous, sentient, wolves, how would the village survive being his enemy? It seemed to Drel that his only option was to accept the aid from this necromancer, and hope for benevolence.

"I don't know that I trust you, Comanatin, but I don't know that that matters. I know Ulter was dead, I was at his funeral, and anyone with the power to bring back the dead will get his way regardless of my decision. I will accept what help you offer, and in return I offer to aid you, within limits."

'Excellent. Lie upon the table Drel, I will begin the procedures immediately.'

It was now that Drel finally noticed how exhausted he was. As he took a step toward the table he staggered unsteadily, his vision swimming. Ulter caught hold of him and led him toward the table, a worried look on his face.

"What's wrong with him?"

Comanatin was pulling tools out of the container by the bed. Each tool he removed flew through the air to hover above his head. Drel could make out no reply from him, but Ulter responded regardless.

"I see. Poor guy's had a rough month. Don't worry Drel, we'll have you better than ever in no time."

As Ulter helped him onto the table Drel got his first good look at the tools that were hovering at the ready. They looked incredibly unpleasant to him, a multitude of blades, saws, and needles, each having a specific and unknown purpose. As Drel lay down, too exhausted to

22

issue any complaint,

he worried for a moment that he had made a mistake. As he began falling asleep his mind concocted horrible possibilities for his future, but he was simply too tired to care. Slowly the imaginings of his mind became less and less coherent, and he never noticed when he finally drifted off.

**

Drel was in total darkness. He tried to bring his hand in front of his face to see it, only to realize he couldn't feel his hands, or the rest of his body for that matter. He felt strangely like a turtle out of its shell. There was a vague recollection at the back of his mind of falling asleep on a table, and he realized he must be dreaming.

As he realized this he saw a source of light in the distance. He tried to move toward it, but with no body, movement seemed impossible. The light seemed brighter than the sun, but didn't seem to illuminate its surroundings. Outside that point of light, there was only darkness.

After a time, he began to notice other lights appearing, some barely visible in the darkness, and others as bright as bonfires, though none seemed so bright as the one in the distance. One of the lights seemed somehow familiar to him. It wasn't very intense, about as bright as a candle, and as he focused on it, the image of a wolf's panting laughter appeared in his head. He distinctly felt this light was somehow that wolf.

Looking away from the wolf light he realized it was in a sort of collection of lights, all similarly bright, and somehow connected, as if by invisible strings. He felt the collection must be a pack of wolves. As he glanced around, he wondered for a moment how he was moving his field of view if he had no body, and he felt suddenly paralyzed. He tried to look around but found he no longer could. He began to fear he would be stuck staring into one point of the darkness forever, but forced himself to calm down, and as he relaxed his vision started shifting again, and he realized how he was doing it. He simply willed his sight to change, and it happened.

He decided to try seeing if he could move in this way, and as he willed himself to see the lights from behind, he suddenly found himself on the opposite side, looking at both the light he had focused on, as well as the lights that were previously behind him.

As he began to experiment with his newfound ability he started to notice more patterns among the lights. Sometimes the groups were all of similar intensity, but other times dim lights were grouped with more intense lights. He saw massive collections of the dimmest of the lights, and as he was examining one he suddenly saw a burst of light to his left, and turning to face it, realized that it was a long trail of light that began somewhere in the unseen distance, and ended directly in front of him. He distinctly felt a sort of invitation from this light, and curious to find out more about it, he accepted.

'Greetings, Drel.'

The voice that suddenly appeared in his mind was distinctly female, despite the lack of sound. He tried speaking the same way he had moved, but willing his thoughts toward the light.

'Not like that, Drel. Think of it simply as speaking, only

with your thoughts instead of your mouth.'

After a few moments of thinking, Drel tried it.
'Like this?'

'Exactly, Drel. I'm surprised to see you so awake and alert, considering the circumstances.'

Drel hesitated a moment. *'How did I get here?'*

'You don't remember getting to the tower? Oh I suppose Comanatin has your senses severed right now. I wonder what kind of hallucinations a lucid mind would have with no stimulus.'

Drel wasn't sure how to respond. *'I don't know about hallucinations, but I'm in the dark, and there are a bunch of lights around me that I think represent creatures.'*

'Interesting. I found you because Comanatin linked you into the collective will of his subordinates. I would imagine you're seeing their individual wills.'

'Does that mean I'm being brought into some sort of collective consciousness?'

The voice paused a moment before responding in detail. *'Consciousness and will are separate. Think of the will as the ties that connect related objects. Your will is the representation of your body and mind, and vice versa. Even abstract ideas have wills, and thus you will find that you have a joint will with your friends, your family, and even members of the same town or nation as yourself. The difference is how strong the connections are, and thus how tangible the will is.'*

'What do I have in common with the other lights, and yourself?'

'I am not a part of this will. I have a connection to Comanatin, and through him, this will. You are bound to it by your bargain with Comanatin.'

Drel was worried by this. *'Did I make the wrong choice when I accepted his deal?'*

The voice hesitated. *'I think Comanatin made the wrong choice in choosing you. But then he and I no longer see eye to eye on such things. As for you, Comanatin has given you a chance to change the world for the better. See to it that you do not disappoint him.'*

Drel suddenly felt lightheaded, and after a moment realized he could feel his body again.

'I suppose Comanatin is waking you up now. I will leave you with one final thought. If you betray him I will make you wish you had never been born.'

Drel opened his eyes to find himself laying upon the table in Comanatin's tower. The room was as sparse as before, and though the only light came from the open door, he found he could see quite clearly. Comanatin stood by the table next to his head, with a woman Drel didn't recognize standing to his left.

The woman was quite tall, and had the lean, muscled build of a woman who did physical labor for a living, but strangely lacked the scars and calluses one would expect. Drel had plenty of his own from accidents in his line of work. She had long, dark hair, and was quite attractive. Drel wondered whether this was the woman who spoke to him in the dream.

As Drel got a bearing on his surroundings he was startled by Comanatin's words appearing in his mind again. Somehow they seemed more familiar now, as if before they were loudly spoken from a great distance, and now were whispered directly in his ear.

'This is Sortira.' The woman by his side bowed slightly. *She will be your mentor until I decide you are prepared to be left to your own devices. I apologize for not explaining more myself, but an unexpected complication has arisen, and I need to act*

immediately.'

"What's going-" Before Drel could even finish his sentence, Comanatin vanished with an odd whooshing sound.

As the sound of Comanatin's exit faded away, Sortira spoke. "He's a busy man, Drel, and we need to get busy as well. Get up, we're going back to the village."

As Drel moved to sit up, he felt very tight, and looking down at his body, found that aside from the long, nasty looking threads of stitching that lined his entire body, he was completely naked. Startled at finding himself nude in the presence of a complete stranger, Drel's eyes darted around the room, looking for his clothes, as he covered his unmentionables with his hands and turned his back toward Sortira.

"They're in the chest. I'm Comanatin's apprentice, Drel. Seeing a naked body isn't going to offend my feminine sensibilities. Put on your clothes and let's go. We're in a hurry."

Drel went over to the chest and took out his clothes. Once he had his underwear on he felt more comfortable, and spoke.

"Why was I naked?"

Sortira laughed "You didn't expect us to perform surgery through your clothes did you?"

"I suppose not. I thought Comanatin performed the procedure on his own. Who are you?"

"I'm Comanatin's apprentice, as I just said. I've learned enough now that he lets me help out during the procedure. It goes faster when he doesn't have to do all the trivial parts by himself. I'm not involved in any of the difficult parts, but I'm learning, and I hope within fifty years or so I'll have learned sufficiently to truly be considered a necromancer."

Drel finished dressing and turned to face her. "Fifty years seems like a long time to learn basic proficiency."

Sortira shrugged and led Drel out the door. "It's actually a very short time period. Comanatin has been doing his research for over a thousand years Drel. He's been a necromancer longer than the history of our civilization. It's a very difficult field. It won't take as long for me to learn as it took him, he really is an excellent teacher."

Drel was shocked. The idea of living for a thousand years was mind boggling. The oldest man in the village was only sixty-two.

"Am I going to live that long?"

Sortira shrugged again as they walked through the forest. "It depends on how careful you are, Drel. Comanatin is the most paranoid person I've ever met, and I've met a few nobles. He doesn't do anything without assessing the risks from every possible angle, and he has more safeguards in place than you would believe. And that's only the ones I know about. As for the potential, yes, you should be able to live indefinitely. Aging is a thing of the past, Drel."

Drel shook his head as he thought it over. "What did you people do to me?"

Sortira laughed. "You sound like you miss the idea of slowing decomposing while still alive. We've deactivated the built-in kill switches that cause you to slowly die over time. We've also adjusted your muscular programming to have a baseline level that can be improved with exercise, but can't be lowered. On top of that we completely rewrote your bodies injury response system. Oh speaking of which, I almost forgot to show you something."

Without skipping a beat, Sortira suddenly turned and punched Drel hard in the arm. Rather than feeling pain, he had a very bizarre sensation he'd never felt before, it felt almost like his body telling him not to repeat that experience, but with no sense of urgency to it. He was too bewildered by the new sensation, and by the sudden attack to respond.

Sortira turned and kept walking, explaining as they went. "That is pain for you now. Comanatin firmly believes that sentient beings don't need a pain center that overrides our rational thoughts. You'll be able to think perfectly clearly while in pain now, and I suggest you use that thinking to prevent further pain."

Drel was rubbing his arm as the odd pain feeling slowly faded away. "So what else is new about me?"

"For now the primary differences are your augmented senses of sight, smell, and touch. The intensities of them aren't changed, so you likely haven't noticed," Drel thought of how he had seen clearly in the near darkness and nodded. "but you will be able to see, feel, and smell with more detail than before. Smell is the hardest to utilize since humans rarely need to rely on it and thus don't pay much attention to it."

Drel pondered. "What about the regeneration and super strength I was told about?"

Sortira laughed. "Not enough to be immortal and have enhanced senses? The other impacts of the procedure won't come until later. Comanatin has planted the seeds, but they have yet to blossom. Over time your entire bodies structure will be rewritten with slightly altered code, but for now you're mostly normal."

"How long will it take?"

Sortira shrugged "Usually it takes a few weeks before the changes take full effect. It depends on how active you are, how well you eat, and things like that. The healthier you are, the faster the changes will take effect. You will notice some slight improvement even over just the next few days, and you'll simply continue to improve until you reach the baseline. From there, it's up to you to improve yourself."

"What do you mean by improving myself?"

Sortira shook her head. "We can get into the will training later. For now let's talk about the current situation. The Ilarans will arrive sometime during the night. Comanatin has other business to attend to, so he won't be involved in the battle, and he's bringing the shamblers with him."

Drel gave her a blank look. "The what?"

"Shamblers are essentially walking corpses. Their minds were lost, and they thus have to have an artificial will set up to-" She paused a moment.

"This is going to take too long to explain Drel. They're walking corpses that can be assigned tasks. In any case. It'll be up to your village to distract the attackers while the immortals deal with them. Your village has a wall which is good, all you need to do is ensure that the villagers are ready to man the walls. The enemy will be expecting you to be unaware of them, so if you can wait to announce your presence until after they're close it will help significantly. Once the enemy is engaged, I and the other immortals will deal with them. If you keep them off the walls, and manage to avoid any arrows that might come your way, nobody will be hurt. Other than the Ilarans, of course."

"How many Ilarans are there?"

Sortira shrugged. "Somewhere between two hundred and two hundred fifty according to the familiars."

"And how many immortals are there?"

Sortira smiled. "About twenty."

Drel rounded on her. "How are twenty people going to take on two hundred? Shouldn't we keep the immortals inside as well and fight them off on the walls?"

Sortira shook her head smugly. "Of course not. Tonight you will see the difference between your average human and an immortal. If we were on the battlements, it wouldn't have as large a mental impact. Just watch and learn."

Drel scowled. "I'm not comfortable with this. If your overconfidence gets my village killed..."

Sortira sighed, and with a movement too quick for him to see, he found himself suspended in the air by the throat, and slammed against a tree. He felt the odd analogue for pain again, and idly wondered how much his body could handle after being cut up and tinkered with so much.

Still effortlessly holding him against the tree, Sortira began speaking. "It's not overconfidence Drel. It's a simple fact. Ilar isn't sending anyone with a powerful will. The crows have confirmed that already. Sveria is involved, but Comanatin will handle her."

She dropped Drel to the ground, where he lay coughing before he recovered enough to choke out. "But

Sveria is a myth."

Sortira shook her head. "There are many myths about Sveria, but the woman herself is no myth. Forget Sveria. Focus on the task at hand. Your only job tonight is to convince your village that enemies are coming."

Drel shook his head "If you immortals can handle this on your own, why do you care how prepared the village is?"

Sortira shrugged, and, helping him off the ground, started moving on. "It will take more than twenty of us to take on the nobility, Drel. This is only the beginning."

Drel nodded. They were planning to use this fight as a display of power. Those who supported them would be encouraged by such a display, and those who didn't...would be terrified. He thought again on her statement that the soldiers were no threat. Was that actually true? He had no way of knowing. In fact there were many things he was in the dark about. Despite all their talk, these immortals said little of substance. First Comanatin, and now Sortira. With this thought he was reminded of the dream, and turned to her.

"Was that you speaking to me in the dream?"

Sortira arched an eyebrow. "Pardon?"

"During the surgery I had a dream, and a woman spoke to me in much the same manner as Comanatin. Was it you?"

Her voice entered his mind, and he could clearly tell it was not the same as the one from the dream. *'No, Drel. I can speak like this, but I did not speak to you during your dream. Given that it was a dream I imagine nobody spoke to you, and it was simply part of the dream.'*

Drel thought a moment. "Will I be able to speak

like that? Is it part of being an immortal?"

She shook her head. "It's not an innate part, no. But the procedure does make it easier. Us immortals are all connected much more intimately than normal humans. If you turn out to be more than just a pretty face, you'll be taught such things."

Drel nodded. They were nearing the village, and he began to think of how he would address them. He didn't want to lie to anyone, but the full situation was unbelievable. He decided to settle on half-truths for now, and explain fully after the battle. More important to him were the strategies for the defense. The walls of the town were short, wooden things, more suited to keep out animals and monsters than humans, and if their intentions were to destroy the town they would likely be prepared to deal with it. Drel did not share Sortira's confidence that the battle would end quickly.

Upon entering the town, they drew quite alot of attention. Drel had been missing for days, and now he was returning with a woman. His friend Corin quickly approached him.

"Drel, you old dog! Here we were about to send out a search party to find you and you come strolling back in with a" His eyes widened in alarm as he came closer, "What happened to your arms?"

Of course he would notice the stitching. Drel's head had recovered fully before he awoke, and most of his body was covered by his clothes, but his bare arms clearly displayed the stitching.

"Nothing too serious, Corin. We need to get the town together immediately though. We have a problem."

Corin muttered to himself. "More problems than

one. Our negotiations fell through the floor with Thelcrest."

Drel shook his head sadly. "It doesn't matter, Corin. You'll understand when I've explained fully."

Corin's eyes widened at this. The negotiations with Thelcrest were critical to keeping Thorlin's Point supplied and healthy. "I'll go gather everyone," he turned and extended a hand to Sortira. "Since my friend here is too dense to have proper manners. I'm Corin." Sortira took his hand, and smiled pleasantly. "Sortira. We have no time for pleasantries, but it is lovely to meet your acquaintance."

Corin nodded, and the three of them began gathering the village in the square. Nobody complained when they learned it was Drel doing the gathering. His disappearance had sparked dozens of rumors ranging from a tryst gone wrong to monsters out of the mountains. Having him come back with a woman matched some of the more sordid rumors, and gathering the village immediately fueled the flames even further. The square was abuzz with gossip as the last people arrived.

Corin came up to Drel again. "That's everyone, Drel. What's your news?"

Drel turned to face the village, and taking a deep breath, began his explanation.

"Thank you everyone for gathering on such short notice. I have some things to say, and we have some preparations to make. This woman is named Sortira. She's a member of a group of fighters called the Immortal," Sortira gave him an odd look, but said nothing. "I'll explain their presence here later, but for now we have work to do. Ilar has sent forces to attack us," the villagers immediately erupted into shocked discussion with their neighbors.

"Please hear me out," the talking quickly stopped, and all eyes were on him.

"The Immortals claim that Ilar is working with Thelryn to eliminate us," Aside from some loud gasps and shocked oaths the village remained silent, listening. "I'm not sure if I believe them, but it's certainly possible. For now we need to focus on our defense. The forces will arrive tonight, and the Immortals have offered their aid. Our task is to hold off a siege of our walls until the Immortals can eliminate the opposing forces. If they fail, we will have to finish the Ilarans off on our own."

Drel took a deep breath. "Here is what needs to happen to ensure our safety tonight. Firstly, our walls and homes are wood. We need to wet them down in advance so it's harder for them to take flame. Verenia," He nodded to a woman in the front row. "You will be in charge of that. Take a group, get it done."

Verenia immediately began quietly assembling a group out of the throng, tapping people on the shoulder and pointing to a gathering point.

"Secondly. Non-combatants need to be kept safe, somewhere in the middle of the village." He nodded to an old man he knew to be capable. "Vorlik. You find a place, and get anyone who isn't fighting over there. Verenia, when you finish with the preparations, make sure you get some water to them just in case."

Verenia looked up from her gathering, nodded, and gave Vorlik a quick smile, before going back to it.

"We don't have alot of time, so we'll need to make this quick. Everyone else will need to collect what weapons they have, and reassemble here. We'll discuss things more then. Get to work everyone."

As if waking from a trance, everyone split apart to do their tasks. Sortira gave him an impressed look.

"Well done, Drel. Why not give them the truth though?"

Drel shook his head. "We'll talk about truth if we're actually attacked tonight, and if we manage to survive it. The situation is too complicated to explain to them right now, and I'm not entirely convinced regardless."

Sortira gave him a long, penetrating look. "It's alot to take in I suppose. Are we going to help with the preparations?"

Drel nodded. "Take me to immortals that will be fighting tonight."

Sortira gave him an odd look. "I don't think you'll be much help with their preparations."

"It doesn't matter. I need to confirm that they're capable of what you say they are, before trusting the lives of my entire village to their success. How the defense is organized will depend on their capabilities."

Sortira nodded slowly. "Fine. I'll have them meet us outside the village."

Drel nodded and began walking toward the front gate. As she matched his pace he turned to ask.

"How long will it take for me to learn the telepathy?"

She shrugged. "Maybe a week, or fifty years, or never."

"That seems like a rather large range."

She sighed heavily. "Most people don't have the

stomach to train their will. It's difficult, and frustrating. Yours is already partially developed toward communication, so I'd imagine it wouldn't take nearly as much work as it took for me, but it will require working at it, and most likely training since you're not aware of your will yet."

Drel took this in. "What do you mean by aware?"

Sortira poked him. "Where did I just touch you?"

"My arm."

She nodded, and suddenly Drel felt a similar sense of violation to the "nightmares" he'd been experiencing for weeks prior to meeting Comanatin. As the feeling faded, she spoke again. "Where did I touch you that time?"

Drel tried to shrug off the feeling. "My mind?"

Sortira shook her head. "Your will. According to Comanatin, some people are easier than others to make aware. He came to control his will naturally, I required a bit of training."

Drel nodded. "Fine. That's something to deal with later."

He picked up the pace, and together they came to the front gate. Waiting just outside were the collected immortals. They all looked very strong, tightly bound muscle covering the frames of both women and men. Their bodies were relatively uniform aside from faces, and the slightly different shapes of the women compared to the men. Drel at first had a difficult time identifying Ulter in the crowd, but gave him a smile when he did.

Sortira spoke up, and as Drel turned his gaze to her he realized she was the only immortal whose build didn't fit the mold. She had similarities to the other immortal women, but she managed to simultaneously look stronger, and more distinctly feminine than the rest. "So what do you want Drel?"

Drel shook his head to dispel the endless parade of questions the scene had instilled in him, then raised his head to respond. "I want to see the two weakest fighters spar."

Sortira arched an eyebrow. "Weakest? It's a relative term I suppose. Orik and Sunter are sloppy. They'll do."

The two immortal men seemed mildly insulted at first, but they came to the front of the group laughing, and took up a battle stance Drel was unfamiliar with.

'Begin'

At the mental signal from Sortira, the two combatants charged each other. At first Drel had difficulty keeping up with the speed of the fight as they lashed at each other over and over, throwing out punches, kicks at a remarkable rate. Slowly his eyes caught up to the fight, however, and he began to make some sense of it. The two combatants were incredibly fast and strong, the force of their attacks often launching their opponent several feet, but Drel could clearly see what Sortira meant by them being sloppy. They seemed to be trained in some sort of martial art, and often attempted to counter each others attacks, but their movements were jerky and ultimately unsuccessful when they tried anything more complicated than simple punches and kicks. It was as if they thought of the maneuvers as something flashy to show off, as opposed to really incorporating them into their strategy. After a few minutes of going back and forth, Orik managed to kick Sunter so hard he hit a tree with a sharp cracking noise, and the felled man surrendered.

Drel rushed over to Sunter to see if he was ok, but Orik was faster, and immediately helped Sunter up. By their laughter, Drel could tell that Sunter was fine. As he reached the tree the immortal had hit, he saw a fracture in the trunk that alarmed him. It was not a small tree, and causing this kind of collateral damage was terrifying. He immediately wondered at the structural integrity of the walls of the village. Before returning to where Sortira stood he turned to the fighters.

"Thank you for your demonstration, men. I have a much better idea of what to expect tonight now."

As he returned to Sortira, he noticed she was scowling. "Even sloppier than usual tonight. They're not used to having an audience. As you can see though, even those two slackers would have no trouble with some poorly trained soldiers. You have nothing to worry about."

Drel nodded. In the close quarters of the woods, he couldn't imagine fighting someone as strong as those two. He had a sudden thought, however, and picking up a nearby branch, walked up to Orik.

"That was an excellent kick you landed there at the end, Orik. I'm impre-" suddenly Drel swung the branch toward Orik's chest as hard as he could manage, only to find his arm caught halfway in Orik's vicelike grip, and his own momentum used to toss him bodily to the ground.

Drel got back to his feet amidst the laughter of the immortals. Orik was giving him an odd look somewhere between amusement and confusion, with a touch of wariness. Drel gave him a smile to ease his mind.

"Sorry about that Orik, I wanted to see just how fast your reflexes were. I figured there was no way I'd be able to hurt you. Thank you very much for your help, and for allowing me to see your abilities first hand before tonight."

After saying their farewells, Drel and Sortira turned back toward the village.

When the other immortals were out of earshot, Drel turned to Sortira. "I believe you now that they won't have any issues with the soldiers. I still have some concerns though."

Sortira nodded. "Collateral damage?"

"Yeah. Our wall is made of the same wood as that tree. Are they going to be tossing people around the way Orik launched Sunter?"

Sortira shook her head. "The two of them are clumsy, but a kick like that would kill a normal person. We're planning to incapacitate, remember. It'll be all grapples, trust me."

Drel nodded. Even taken by surprise Orik didn't have any trouble keeping up with Drel's attack and completely neutralizing it. He was reasonably confident now that the immortals could do what they claimed. All that remained now was to help the village prepare as best he could.

**

That night a lone rider rode through the dark forest on the road to Thorlin's Point. The rider wore a long cloak with the hood up, which utterly concealed their features. As the rider's horse walked along the road, a sudden sound drew both to a halt. It had been a shout, far off in the direction they were heading, and it was quickly followed by more. The rider quickly brought the horse to a gallop in response to the sound, charging down the dark path. After mere moments, however, the rider twisted suddenly in the saddle, laying their body straight across the back of the horse, and pulling it to a stop. The rider pulled a wicked looking dagger from somewhere beneath their cloak, and with a twang, cut the deadline that had almost taken off their head. Looking around slowly, the rider spoke in the arrogant tones of a noblewoman.

"I can feel your presence out there, fools. Come out where I can see you."

There was movement in the trees all around the road, and slowly, dozens of figures moved into the moonlight, barring the return path, while the path toward Thorlin's Point lay open.

"Bandits? No, you have no blood on you...But who..."

A rush of wind caught her attention on the road ahead, and a dark figure appeared, mere feet away from her horse.

"I'm afraid Thorlin's Point is mine, Sveria. You've badly mistreated your toys."

Sveria recognized that voice from somewhere in the distant past. "Comanatin?"

The figure nodded. "Yes. While you've played with your toy kingdom, I've been making my own preparations. It is time for you to stop holding back humanity from its potential."

Sveria laughed. "And so you bring shamblers to

face me? Their lack of blood is an inconvenience, but nothing more. You have plenty to spare, I think it's time for you to bleed for me."

As she said this, a dagger appeared from within her cloak, and flew toward Comanatin, only to pass harmlessly through as though he were nothing but air.

Sveria snarled and dismounted.

"I had forgotten you were an elf, Comanatin. It's been so many centuries now." She removed another dagger from her cloak, and with a quick motion cut a thin line into the flank of her horse. It remained completely stationary, as if it couldn't even feel the wound.

"Now where are you...There!" As the horses blood blackened, another dagger appeared and sailed into the trees on the side of the road, lodging itself to the hilt in one of the thick trunks. Comanatin reappeared, holding up his cloak to look at the hole that had been made.

"You're losing your touch, Sveria, though you've certainly bred yourself an interesting horse. I hadn't counted on that."

Sveria laughed. "Being a noble does have its advantages. It's amazing what you can do with a few centuries of breeding and a bit of obedience training."

Comanatin shook his head. "You forgot one thing though. It is still a horse, with no training of the will."

As he finished his sentence, the horse simply vanished, a woosh of air the only evidence it had ever been there.

Sveria cursed, and charged Comanatin as twin daggers appeared in her hands. He dodged deftly, and with a wooshing sound, disappeared again. This time Sveria was prepared, and threw a dagger in the direction he reappeared, only to curse as it sunk deeply into the flesh of one of the shamblers. As if on cue, the woods came alive again, and all of the shamblers began to advance upon her. Snarling with rage, she tried to cut a path to the necromancer through the shambling corpses. With inhuman strength, her blades cut through tissue and bone alike, cleaving heads and limbs from their unliving bodies as she dodged their feeble attacks. Nothing stopped them, however. As she became more and more mired in the fight with those ahead, more advanced from behind, and not wanting to be cornered, she deftly dodged her way out of the fray.

Comanatin was nowhere in sight, but she could hear his voice clearly, seeming to come in on a breeze. "Give up Sveria. You can't win without any blood."

Sveria snarled again. "I won't run from a coward like you."

"Are you still angry about that? I didn't flee, I simply stopped offering my services to those who didn't appreciate them."

Sveria laughed. "And now? You can't hide behind your illusions and corpses forever, elf."

Sveria took one of her daggers, and cut a line down the back of her arm as the shamblers continued their advance toward her. The blood from the wound coalesced into a red blade, which hovered beside her, before launching itself at the army of shamblers. One by one it sliced into them, cutting off limbs and heads, working to systematically incapacitate them as she kept her distance. A sudden kick caught her off guard as it crashed into her from behind and knocked her to the ground. As she stood up, painfully aware of the bruising she would have from such a blow, she saw Comanatin standing on the path near her previous location, before he disappeared again.

"The bastard is toying with me," She thought, and as another invisible kick drove her to the ground again, she realized she wouldn't be able to defeat him in her current state. She recalled her blade from its work with the shamblers, and focusing on her wound to determine Comanatin's location, began charging down the road toward Thorlin's Point.

Comanatin followed behind her, but made no effort to teleport in front and stop her. She could still feel his location, and thought it odd until she came across a turn in the road, and had to dodge to the side suddenly to avoid the blade that came slashing down toward her head. A swarm of skeletal shamblers covered the road in front of her, and seemed to spread deep into the woods as well. She ducked as Comanatin teleported in and launched a kick toward her head, and then sprinted south through the woods, deciding to simply escape.

Comanatin had won this round. He had prepared for her coming in advance, knowing full well what he would be up against, and she had fallen into the trap. He followed closely, but without his shamblers to distract her, didn't pursue his attacks. As she fled the forest she heard his parting words.

"The humans are mine now, Sveria. You would do well to flee and never return."

**

The battle ended nearly before it began. As the attackers began their assault Drel signalled the other villagers, who lit their torches, engulfing the area in blinding light. At the same time the immortals came upon the attackers, and began dismantling their force from behind. Within minutes those attackers that were still standing surrendered, certain that monsters had descended upon them out of the dark.

Drel was watching now, as Sortira tended to the wounded. Most of the Ilarans had dislocated shoulders or other joints, and she or another immortal would simply wrench them back in place, but some had fallen badly, and had breaks or fractures. For these she would feel the area with her hands, and with a mixture of rubbing motions and periods of apparent concentration, fix the bone.

The Ilarans were being sent to the town hall under guard after being checked over by Sortira. After roughly half of them had been healed and sent off, Comanatin appeared next to her with a rush of wind. Almost as soon as he arrived, the soldiers began eliciting shocked gasps one by one in the line, and moving their arms or legs tentatively, stood cured and bewildered. Drel looked on in awe himself. Sortira's healing was miraculous in its own right, but was at least visible and to an extent understandable. Comanatin wasn't even looking at the men he was healing. It was otherworldly. Within a minute, Comanatin nodded, and the remaining soldiers were led to the town hall by a group of immortals.

'The first step has been taken, but complications have arisen. Sveria will return soon, and we must be prepared for her arrival. Your training will begin immediately. Come, Drel, Sortira. It is time to prepare for war.'

As Drel took Comanatin's outstretched hand, he realized his world had changed forever. No longer would he and his people lay helpless before the fickle politics of the nobility. The power to defend themselves was in their grasp, they simply had to reach out and take it.

The revolution had begun.

The Immortal Revolution

Latilya Sivar

The reaction to my previous work was somewhat mixed within Midgar. Some rightly made the connection between the woodcutter Drel, and Sordrel the Deceiver, from the original tale, and felt I painted him in too positive a light. I stand by my decision to tell the story of Drel, as my ancestor felt it was important enough to record in his own collections, and I believe it is necessary to truly understand what follows.

Nobody is entirely sure what happened after the end of the battle for Thorlin's Point, where Drel made the fateful decision to join with the immortals, and the necromancer that led them. What is known is that within weeks, contact with the lumber towns of Thelcrest and Ilcrest was lost, and a group who called themselves immortals was recruiting for a revolution in Thelryn and Ilar. The leader of this band called himself Sordrel.

The impact of the initial uprising was quite dramatic. The flames of revolution spread quickly, and the immortals were gaining recruits rapidly. Nobles throughout the region were scrambling to get information about this threat to their rule, and determine how to exploit it for personal gain. I get ahead of myself, however. This is where my ancestor, Varan, enters the picture.

Varan was a spy in the employ of Lord Greis of Varngrim. At the time Varngrim was a trade hub within the lands of men, and the nobility there had a vested interest in the stability of the region. News of the trouble in Ilar and Thelryn had reached Varngrim by now, and Lord Greis had called upon Varan to discuss the issue.

As Varan entered his lord's study, he was surprised to find that Lord Greis was already there. Lord Greis was an incredibly busy man, and he never sat in one place for long. He was perpetually late for appointments not as part of some power game to ensure servants knew their place, as was popular with so many other nobles, but rather because he was always on the move keeping his dominion under control.

"I apologize for keeping you, my lord." Varan said humbly, bowing deeply as the guard let himself out and closed the door behind him.

Lord Greis maintained a scowl only until the guard had left, and his scolding was relatively minor. "You're not late, however I arrived first. This is unacceptable. In any case, I called upon you to discuss your new genealogy. How is it progressing?"

Varan smiled, enjoying the game. He put a lot of effort into ensuring his histories and genealogies were the most boring in the world, and he knew why Lord Greis had truly summoned him. "My progress goes quite well sir, however Cilar has been a guard long enough to know how boring my tales are. He went to the other end of the hall to talk to Hercick about one of the new maids as soon as he let me in. There's no need for the preamble."

Lord Greis nodded, and then smiled openly. "You have truly remarkable care, Varan. I'm always reminded what a boon your services are to me."

Varan laughed. "Which services would that be, my lord? The royalties you receive for the most boring books in the land, or the information you receive from your spy?"

Lord Greis laughed as well. "I think you can guess, Varan." His voice became more serious. "Surely you're aware of the trouble in the north by now?"

Varan nodded. It was common knowledge that the north was dealing with some sort of cult, and less well known that Lady Cruor was involved somehow, but the details were sketchy at this point, with nothing but the wild rumors of merchants to fall back upon.

Lord Greis continued. "Lady Cruor appears to have gone mad. I just received word that she has taken it upon herself to declare war on Thorlin's Point, claiming that there is a death cult based in the town led by some sort of necromancer."

Varan scoffed. "A necromancer? Lady Cruor wouldn't believe a fairytale like that. Her mind is like a vice."

Lord Greis Shrugged. "Lady Cruor has always been a very shrewd woman. I would trust nothing she says at face value. However she is also quite old by now. She was well established in politics before I was born. Perhaps she has finally lost her mind."

Varan nodded. "She may have caught some

disease of the mind, but I find it more likely she's making a political move that's beyond us. The cult may very well be of her own devising. I assume you want me to head for Thelryn without delay? What are my priorities in this?"

Lord Greis laughed. "Your priorities are the same as always, my friend. My interests. I trust you to know how best to protect them. If Lady Cruor has truly descended into madness she can't be allowed to bring us with her. If she has not, and this is some scheme of hers, I expect you to find out what it is, and get us in on it. If she can take advantage of this, then so can we. Keep an open mind and do what you do best, Varan. You have my authority to hire Relin if you think they're necessary."

Varan nodded and noted that the conversation outside had changed topic to the rumors about the cult, though it was nothing he hadn't heard before. "I assume my transport is waiting?"

Lord Greis nodded. "I've made all the necessary arrangements. Given that you've met Lady Cruor, I've made no attempt to give you an alias. You requested a trip to Thelryn as a chance to do some research for your new book, and I graciously allowed it."

Varan nodded, and smiled. "My ulterior motive is that the Thelryn countryside is absolutely beautiful, and I long to hear the singing flowers again. You, of course, have no idea."

Lord Greis laughed. "Quite. I trust that thanks to your meddling, I shall come out of this richer than I went in."

Varan chuckled. "Of course my lord. My every move shall rain gold down upon you."

Lord Greis gave Varan a dismissive wave through

his laughter. "I've come to expect nothing less. Good luck my friend."

Varan turned to the door, and let himself out. The guards were still gossiping as he left. As Varan traveled through the hallways of the mansion, he began to listen in on conversations out of habit, and was amazed to find that the gossip throughout the entire house revolved around the rumors from the north. The rumors had only started a few days ago, but they'd grown more exaggerated and ridiculous with each passing day.

One conversation in particular caught his ear. A servant was whispering a new rumor to a friend, one that even Varan had not yet heard.

"It's the crows. They're the eyes of the necromancer. My gran told me. Watch out for them, and close your shutters at night so they don't come in to steal your soul."

Upon hearing it, Varan knew it would be a popular rumor. Nobody would ask why the man's grandmother knew anything about monsters long since destroyed, though there would be thousands of questions of what a necromancer was, and likely hundreds of answers given.

Varan had heard many legends, and some histories, that related the tale of the necromancers. Back before the lands of men were cleansed of monsters, there were a pair of creatures known as necromancers who resided within. These creatures looked much akin to men, aside from identifiable characteristics that changed from story to story. Usually horns, pointed ears, a tail, or some other bestial characteristic. The necromancers both worked with the dead, however they differed on how to do so. One necromancer focused its skills on the reanimation of the body, and created legions of soulless husks which it used to destroy its enemies. The other necromancer focused on the reanimation of the soul, and it thus had legions of chained ghosts which could drain the very life force from their enemies. During The Culling, the enormous war to cleanse the valley of monsters, the two necromancers fought for a time on the side of the humans, thinking to eliminate their monstrous competitors, and dominate humanity once the rest of the monsters were slain. After a time, however, the two began to quarrel about which of their magics was superior, and they began a battle which slew them both, their armies disintegrating with the deaths of their masters.

As he left the mansion, he noted a large crow on the roof, quite near the chambers he met with Lord Greis. He had been seeing the crows more and more of late, and chuckled as he thought of the rumor he had just heard. He was surprised by how popular the rumors had become. He supposed everyone loved a good monster story, and what better villains than useless scavengers like crows? As he began his journey to the north he wondered what plot was involved here, and who was responsible for the ridiculous monster stories that were spreading throughout the populace like wildfire.

**

'Your little war seems to be going well, Comanatin. But why didn't you kill Sveria when you had the chance?'

'I saw no need to be reckless. I can keep her under control from here, and it would be a shame to have to kill such a remarkable

specimen regardless.'

'You do realize she's now in a city with thousands of blood sacks to draw upon don't you?'

'Oh yes, and she'll be loathe to leave without an army now. In fact, she seems rather reluctant to attack my diplomats. Sordrel has been openly recruiting there for days.'

'She realizes that any that join you are just more fuel for her magic. How are you planning to handle the inevitable battles to come? Your quaintly named immortals would only be a liability against her.'

'I already told you I have no intention of getting involved in large scale battles with her. If she wants to believe I'm starting the war of the millenia it will only help my cause.'

'Then what are you recruiting for? You haven't even finished converting the people of the forest, why keep so many liabilities around that you'll need to feed?'

'I need more competent leaders. Sortira has never been interested in a leadership role, but until Sordrel came along I had nobody else to delegate to. Your average human is completely unqualified, so I need a larger pool to draw upon. I'll be sending those who don't make the cut back out as diplomats.'

'Won't the guards simply kill them? The immortals can handle some human guardsmen, but your typical merchant will simply be executed for treason.'

'Sordrel is quite talented. I fully expect to have control of the guards in Thelryn within the week. Many of my new recruits come out of the military. As I secure new cities, the immortals will move on to the more dangerous areas.'

'Wouldn't it be simpler to just deal with Sveria and then take the cities by force? It's not like the humans could possibly stop you, and there would likely be less bloodshed.'

'It is important that the humans think they have a choice

in this. Playing the role of protector is far simpler than the role of tyrant. By creating a revolution, rather than simply conquering, I shall have far less work in securing the empire I need to reach my goals.'

'I still think you underestimate the mindless violence of humanity, Comanatin. By using humans rather than shamblers you're giving up control of the situation.'

'I know, Gingko, but I believe the results will be worth it. Far too many promising individuals are held back from reaching their potential, or slaughtered before they have a chance to shine. Even you must admit that the natural talents of a truly living creature are nigh impossible to replicate.'

'Wraith and Shade are far more powerful and intelligent than any human.'

'Even yourself? Or have you forgotten?'

'Don't give me that, Comanatin. We both know your average human is nothing like me.'

'But how can you find the outliers if you allow them to perish in obscurity?'

'They wouldn't be obscure if they were like me. This argument will go nowhere, old friend. If there's no other news I should get back to my research into imbued pyromancy. It's a remarkably rare trait and finding suitable test subjects is difficult.'

'Isn't that trait relatively common among dragons?'

'It is, but dragons make horrible test subjects. They're far too powerful to keep comfortably under control, and their wills are near impossible to navigate without causing permanent damage. They have useful parts, but useless wills. Besides, I finally have some peace and quiet for once. I have no interest in starting another war with the dragons by stealing test subjects.'

'I wouldn't dream of suggesting it. We should compare our recent results soon. These little wars of ours keep distracting our

attention away from more interesting things.'

'I'd like that. Farewell for now, old friend.'

'Farewell, Gingko'

**

As Varan started out from the northern gate of the city, he decided his best bet would be to try to infiltrate the cult, rebellion, or gang that these rumors were based on. Looking back, he noted a pair of crows sitting on the ramparts above either side of the gate, observing the road below them. The crows truly had been acting strange of late. Until recently they tended to collect in large groups, the racket of their gatherings was truly remarkable. Recently, however, he had noticed that they seemed to be becoming more and more spread out. There were hardly ever no crows to be found if he looked, but he rarely saw large gatherings anymore. He idly wondered what could have changed their long standing habits as he rode along the road to the north.

He made a game of spotting crows in eaves, trees, and on buildings as he went. They appeared to be going about their business as normal despite their spontaneous antisocial behavior. He thought perhaps they had simply gotten tired of stealing from each other. By midmorning, he had passed far enough from Varngrim that the residences were thinning out, and by afternoon he came across the first patch of singing flowers, bringing a reminiscent smile to his face.

Varan had loved the singing flowers since he was a child. The beautiful plants appealed to him on multiple levels, and he always delighted in hearing and seeing them.

When he was very young his father explained that the singing of the flowers was in truth the wind blowing through an intricate system of stems and roots that sounded like wordless singing. What his father could never explain was how the collections of flowers always seemed to sound like a chorus rather than a cacophony. Varan would lie in fields for hours as a child, simply listening to the chorus, and trying to find the pattern that explained it.

Unfortunately, the singing flowers were considered weeds by most people. The singing was pleasant, but continuous, and few people wanted to live with the noise right in their backyard. The farmers in the south destroyed them to make room for their crops, and most of the central region was too urban. It was only when he headed north toward Ilar and Thelryn that he got to hear the music from his childhood. As he continued north, he let his troubles disappear for a short while, and simply lost himself in the song and beauty around him.

**

It was immediately obvious upon arriving at Thelryn that things were not well in the city. The southern gate was heavily guarded, and a long inspection line had formed as if they were searching people for illicit goods. Talking to the people in line, it became clear the guards were searching for cultists, and that anybody they deemed to be suspiciously strong was being locked up. Varan wasn't quite sure what was meant by suspiciously strong, but he worried that his profession as scribe wouldn't match his build. He had a rather strict training regimen in case he ran into trouble on the job, and thus had a rather strong build. Your typical historian led a cushy life, and tended to develop a rather round body because of it. As a traveling historian it was well within character to be in shape, but he decided it would be silly to tempt fate with the guards when he knew an easier way in.

As he turned to leave, however there was a sudden uproar inside the city, and he made out the sounds of a large group heading toward the gate. The guards pushed the crowd outside the gates, before re-entering the city and slamming the gates shut behind them. For a short while, all Varan could make out above the sounds of the crowd outside were the indistinct sounds of the approaching group, punctuated by the occasional clatter of a halberd hitting the ground or a wall. Shortly, however, he heard a clear, pleasant voice, speaking loudly so as to be heard, but not shouting.

"Hello officer. Glad to see you still have a job after yesterday. Would you be so kind as to open the gate?"

The low voice of the officer on duty was barely perceptible through the heavy gate. "We're not opening the gate for you monsters. I don't care how silver your tongue, creature."

There came a remorseful sigh. "Very well, officer. We'll open the gate ourselves."

Suddenly there was an enormous clatter, as bodies and halberds hit the floor on the other side of the gate, and in a few moments the gate began to open, revealing a group of powerful figures led by a rather large, smiling man. He wore no shirt, displaying an impressive array of muscles to the world at large. Varan now understood what the guards meant by suspiciously muscular. The man's build was large, but perfectly proportioned, with no muscle group out of sync. He had an attractive, friendly face, and as he glanced at the fallen soldiers around him, a mischievous smirk touched his lips.

"I apologize for the delay everyone. We seem to have upset the nobility and they insisted on setting these poor men against us." He nodded toward the guardsmen. "I'd love to stay and chat, but we have some people in need of protection here," he nodded toward the large collection of peasants and merchants that Varan had assumed were spectators, "so we really need to get going. If any of you want to join the revolution against the noble tyrants, come with us!"

With that he set off at a brisk, but not rushed pace, and the crowd outside parted readily for him. Varan contemplated for a moment following the man, and noted that many of the people in the crowd outside had the same idea. The crowd thinned considerably as the new recruits passed. Varan shrugged away the thought, however. He needed to get some information before he could attempt his infiltration. The man did seem remarkably pleasant, however. He looked every bit the hero ready to sweep away villainy.

Varan shook his head. Regardless of how charismatic he was, the man was dangerously deluded to think he could lead a successful rebellion. Varan considered getting Relin involved immediately, but decided against it. A little instability could be incredibly profitable if Lord Greis took proper advantage, and it wasn't allowed to go too far. He wondered what Lady Cruor was planning with this young revolutionary.

As the rebels grew further from the town, the guards began picking themselves up off the ground, muttering and cursing to themselves. The crowd had dispersed by now, either leaving with the revolutionaries or taking advantage of the situation to get into the city unmolested by the guards. Varan approached the man who appeared to be in command.

"Hello officer. Is the checkpoint still in effect?"

The officer grunted in disgust. "It's a waste of time but the nobles insist. Everyone knows the bastards fly over the walls as crows. They're monsters, not men."

Varan was taken aback for a moment by his tone. "As crows you say?"

The officer looked utterly exhausted, and beyond hope. He didn't appear to be injured, nor were any of the other guardsmen. Why then were they all laying prone when the gates opened? Were they complicit in the rebellion? If so the man was an excellent actor. After a long sigh the officer nodded and waved Varan into the city. "I don't have time to waste on common knowledge. You'll learn soon enough."

Varan looked to the other guardsmen and saw their leader's despair reflected in their eyes. He also noted that there appeared to be fewer of them than were on the ground before. Had some run off? Or had they joined the revolutionaries outright? As Varan headed into the city, he worried for the first time that these rebels could very well cause total anarchy if left unchecked. What were the nobles here in Thelryn thinking allowing this to happen?

Varan decided that if the rebels had already made this much progress something needed to be done. He needed to infiltrate their camp immediately, and he didn't have time to gather information in the city first. He had traveled light, with only the tools of his trade as a scribe. Varan said his farewells to the guards, and headed immediately for the home his master kept for his visits, and left the city through the secret passage he had earlier considered entering from.

**

Lady Cruor was having a good day. The preparations for her battle with Comanatin were going slowly, but the recent intrusions by the immortals had sped things up considerably. The fact that the immortals were quite successful with their recruitment served only to delight her. The other nobles were in a panic about the town guard being so helpless, and were throwing their soldiers into the newly formed task force to destroy the source of the incursions. Comanatin's minions were recruiting mostly the poor and useless dregs of society, so Lady Cruor didn't mind their treason in the slightest. Unlike some of the other nobles, she held no illusions that the peasants were loyal. She knew all too well about the treachery of mortals. These dark thoughts were dispelled as knocks came at the door.

"What is it?"

The guard outside called in "It's Cedrik, milady. He says he has information you requested."

"Ah good, let him in, Lor."

Cedrik entered the room with his head bowed in subservience.

"I'm sorry to bother you milady, but you asked me to inform you if certain individuals entered the city, and we've received word that Lord Greis's scribe Varan has just arrived."

Lady Cruor nodded. "Greis always was fast to react to news. Very well. Keep an eye on the residence. I want to know where he goes and who he talks to."

Cedrik bowed deeply. "Of course, milady. I already took the liberty of arranging a watch given your interest. He appears to have taken the day to rest. What behaviors shall we remain on the lookout for?"

"I want to know if he speaks to anyone else on the watch list, as well as know any dealings he has with smugglers, assassins, or other groups. The situation in the north is delicate, and though I don't expect Greis's spy to do anything rash, times such as these can influence people to strange actions. I also want to know immediately if he has left the city."

Cedrik nodded. "We've been unable to plant a spy in his household, milady. If they have a tunnel we'll be unable to identify his departure immediately. I'll keep you informed of any suspicious absences. Given his persona it is not out of character to take a day of rest after traveling, but he may have already left the city."

Lady Cruor smiled. "It's of no consequence. If he doesn't show his face by tomorrow afternoon inform the staff at the household that I request a meeting. That will both tell us whether he has left, as well as ensure his immediate presence when he returns. Keep a close eye on Relin. We don't want anyone talking to him without our knowledge."

"Him, milady?"

Lady Cruor gave him an odd look. "It's both the name of the group, and the leader. Do keep up." Her tone hardened. "Keep me informed, Cedrik, you're dismissed."

Cedrik gave a hasty bow, and retreated from the room. He knew he had spoken out of turn, and that was a very dangerous thing to do around a woman like Lady Sveria Cruor.

**

Finding the rebels proved to be a rather simple task for Varan. They had simply gone around the city, then followed the road north from there, making no attempt to hide or rush. He came upon their camp in the evening. As the group of refugees from the city sat around the camp fire eating their dinners, the leader of the rebels, still inexplicably shirtless, was telling a story. There appeared to be nobody standing watch, and as Varan came closer he began to make out what the leader was saying.

"And so, my heavily intoxicated friend, who shall remain nameless, was in the process of picking a fight with the behemoth of a man thrice his size when-"

The leader appeared to notice Varan for the first time, as he entered the ring of light, though the twinkle in his eye indicated to Varan that he was expected. "Oh I see we have another guest at our table. Are you here to join the revolution or are you simply a traveler on his way north?"

Varan had arranged his reply in advance. "Neither actually. I'm a historian and your rebellion is the first to last more than an hour in centuries. I came to learn more about it."

The leader smiled at Varan warmly. "Well most of us here are illiterate, so we don't read many histories, but you're welcome to stay with us, share our food and fire, and write whatever you please. In fact, I've spent all night talking and haven't eaten yet. Come, share a meal with me and we can talk about your profession. It wouldn't hurt to have more educated men in our ranks."

Varan knew better than to reject an offered meal. People could be touchy when their hospitality was spurned. After grabbing the bowl offered to him by one of the refugees, Varan sat down next to the leader.

"Thank you for sharing your food. My name is Varan. I assume you're the leader of this revolution? How should I address you?"

The leader smiled cheerfully. "My name is Sordrel, and there's no need for honorifics here. I was a woodcutter in Thorlin's Point before the nobility decided to declare war on us. Now I'm just taking advantage of the opportunity offered by the immortals to free everyone from tyranny."

Varan had heard rumors that Ilar was getting impatient with Thelryn over the Thorlin's Point situation, but he had chalked it up to more silly posturing. Ilar and Thelryn were always angry with each other about something.

"How can you declare war on your own vassals?"

Sordrel laughed bitterly. "By sending an army to slaughter them."

Varan was more surprised that he hadn't heard about it, than the act itself. Annihilating Thorlin's Point entirely would go a long way toward stabilizing relations between the two city-states. It was exactly the kind of thing he would expect. As he thought about it the fact that it didn't surprise him disturbed him greatly.

"I see. I'm sorry for your loss. But-"

Varan stopped as he saw Sordrel was laughing. "Loss? Oh no. We defended our village, thanks to the immortals. The nobility is about to understand how it feels to be powerless. We will rally the people against their oppression, and take back this land for all of humanity, not merely a few.

"So you intend to overthrow the government in Thelryn?"

"Not just Thelryn. Ilar will follow shortly thereafter, and the flames of revolution will spread until the very idea of noble blood has been purged from this land."

Varan was shocked. "You plan to kill all the nobles?"

Sordrel laughed. "There's no need. When their wealth and influence are gone, they will simply be welcomed as people, not as nobles. Some will need to be brought to justice. The crimes and abuses of power some nobles are notorious for need to be punished, however the rest will simply be brought into the fold."

Varan nodded slowly. The words would have sounded crazy coming from anyone else. The idea that a small town like Thorlin's Point had the resources necessary to challenge the combined forces the nobles could field was ludicrous, and yet... No. He wasn't sure where the idea that if anyone could pull it off it was this man came from, but he knew it wasn't his own mind. He didn't think that way. He began to feel distinctly uncomfortable, as if his mind weren't entirely his own.

Sordrel appeared to notice Varan's discomfort, and put a hand on his shoulder.

"Are you alright? I apologize for my preachy outburst. It's part of my job to be a bit overly enthusiastic. I'll leave you to finish your meal in peace, if you need anything just ask me or any of the other immortals. You're welcome to join us on our return trip to Thorlin's Point if you'd like. I can guarantee you safe passage there and back, and I just know as a historian-" The man laughed suddenly, and Varan got the distinct impression that Sordrel knew his reasons for being here. "You'll be very interested in seeing how we plan to win."

Varan nodded absently. He felt lightheaded and confused. It wasn't out of the ordinary for an odd thought to enter his head that seemed out of place or silly, but this was different. It felt distinctly as if his mind was being tampered with, and he didn't like it. It was ridiculous, he knew, but he couldn't shake the thought of someone tinkering with his brain. He decided he wasn't going to get anything productive done second guessing his every thought, and decided to get some sleep. After lying down he thought he could distantly hear the sound of the singing flowers over the sounds of the camp, and he smiled as he descended into blissful slumber.

**

Sordrel was staring into the dying fire as the light of dawn first began lightening the horizon. He hadn't slept much since his body finished the changes that made him an immortal. It was another change to get used to. He could sleep whenever he wanted, but his body and mind simply needed it less, and there was so much to do that he tended to forget for days at a time. Comanatin and

Sortira both scolded him when he went long enough to impair his ability to function, and he supposed it was just another skill he would have to learn. As he tried to remember how many days it had been since he slept, Comanatin contacted him.

'Are you ready to learn proper control of your ability now?'

'I don't understand. Isn't it enough to do my best and try to convince people without magical tricks? We're in the right; we shouldn't need to coerce people magically.'

'If you don't want to coerce people magically you need to learn control, Sordrel. You can't stop it if you don't understand it. I think what truly worries you is learning what people are really like. As long as your subtle manipulations are in place your well made arguments can sway them readily, but as soon as you stop using your power people will shell up and defend their fallacies to their dying breath.'

'I don't believe that.'

'Then prove it. Learn control, so you can see first-hand the difference. You have power, but instead of wielding it you allow it to wield you. You can't afford that in the presence of other people with developed wills and minds. Varan's discomfort last night was due to your will tinkering when his defenses were up. He hasn't seen the power we wield yet. He likely thinks you're an addled but dangerous peasant, and is confused how someone so overconfident could have successfully escaped the city. These thoughts work against your will, and in someone like him, the conflict between his true thoughts, and the thoughts your will is trying to place there, creates strife.'

'I thought my will was supposed to be subtle?'

'It is subtle, but it is also uncontrolled. When you try to convince someone with a developed will that the sky is brown not only will they disagree, but in addition your will's attempts at manipulation will stand out plainly. Imagine a thief shrouded in

darkness in broad daylight.'

'Why haven't I run into this before?'

'You have. Sortira complains often about that intrusive will of yours. She knows what you're capable of and can defend herself from your manipulations, but it's irritating for her.'

'And you?'

'I have dealt with far more powerful intrusions than your own, Sordrel. If your will is like an annoying fly to Sortira, for me it is more akin to a mote of dust. Hardly something to actively think about.'

'What about the dozens of other people I interact with daily?'

'Varan is the first non-immortal you have met with a will on par with your own. His is actually far more developed in some ways. He is paranoid and hard working in a way that you are not. Despite his lack of awareness of his will he does an excellent job of training it. If you were to whisper along with the thoughts you send as you used to, he could likely hear you from where he lies at this moment.'

Sordrel looked over toward Varan, on the other side of the camp. He was lying in apparent slumber amidst the crowd of recruits who had partied themselves to sleep the night before.

'How did he manage to sleep with the ruckus last night if his hearing is that sharp?'

'Control, Sordrel. He has control.'

**

As Varan woke, he took in the sounds of the camp. He had trained himself long ago to wake up inconspicuously and alert. The camp was quiet, with only the sounds of methodical breathing, and the occasional small movement to be heard. Recognizing no immediate threats, he went through his mental exercises, reinforcing the character he would be playing today.

Today he was Varan the historian. He was a well-meaning, but somewhat befuddled man, who had made the decision to follow the rebels because it seemed like the sort of thing a historian should take an active interest in. He tended to follow rules, and couldn't quite understand those who did not, though he bore them no animosity. He decided his conversation last night was well within character, and that he would explain his sudden strange behavior as travel fatigue. He had been on the road several days after all. He still wasn't sure what happened, but he shrugged it off as his paranoia getting the best of him.

As he opened his eyes and looked around, he noticed that the only immortal still in the camp was the leader, Sordrel, who was sitting on the ground staring into the firelight. The refugees appeared to be asleep. Varan picked his way over to where Sordrel was sitting,

"Good morning, Sordrel. You're up early."

Sordrel nodded toward the fire, apparently lost in thought, then suddenly looked up and smiled at Varan.

"Good morning, Varan. You went to bed early last night and missed the party. I have no idea how you slept through the ruckus."

Varan laughed. "Living with nobles you get used to sleeping around wild parties. They don't have much better to do with their time."

"You aren't invited to the parties?"

"I'm too busy for parties. The genealogies don't write themselves you know. Each entry needs to be carefully checked and double checked to ensure accuracy. I wouldn't have gotten where I am today if I allowed myself to be distracted by pleasantries."

Sordrel laughed. "To me, life is all about the pleasantries. So what brought you up to Thelryn? You live in Varngrim, don't you?"

Varan nodded pleasantly, but internally he questioned how this man knew his residence. Sordrel had implied he was illiterate the night before, and Varan had made no mention of his Lord or his home. He decided to take a risk and see if it caused a reaction.

"I do indeed! I came to gather information on the Cruor family." Sordrel didn't appear to react at all to the name. "Would you believe there isn't a single record tracing their family line? It's a travesty."

Sordrel shrugged. "I don't know any of the noble families in Thelryn. In Thorlin's Point, we never paid much attention to politics. It was too far removed to be relevant." He paused a moment. "Or so we thought, anyway."

Varan nodded sadly. "History is important to everyone, my friend. Did you know that your rebellion is the first act of treason to go unchecked for more than a day in hundreds of years? It's a rather remarkable achievement, regardless of politics. How did you manage to defeat the city guards with so few of you, and unarmed no less?"

Sordrel smiled mischievously. "We have our ways. Becoming an immortal makes you physically superior to your average person. I was a reasonably strong guy to begin with, but if I wanted to fell a tree now, I wouldn't need an axe."

71

Varan lifted an eyebrow. "That's quite a claim. You've mentioned the immortals before. Does the name of your group hold a particular significance? I assume you all have some sort of training regime?"

Sordrel shook his head. "It's not that simple, Varan. We're fundamentally unlike other humans. We've been given a leg up in achieving the limits of human potential. Assuming there truly are limits."

Varan nodded blankly, but internally he was thinking of the rumors that these weren't men at all, but were monsters in disguise. "And how did you get this leg up?"

Sordrel smiled. "Just a little minor surgery." He shrugged. "You have your own abilities that set you apart from the rest of humanity don't you? The rest of us are all deaf and blind compared to you, aren't we?"

Varan started a bit. This was an unexpected swing in the conversation. "I'm not sure what you mean. Obviously some people don't pay particular attention to their surroundings, but I'd hardly say they're either deaf or blind."

Sordrel laughed. "I know about your perceptiveness, Varan. One might call it unnatural to overhear conversations held in a sealed room from half a castle away. It's part of what makes you such an excellent spy."

Varan laughed easily, but internally he was rattled. It was common for his marks to think he was a spy initially, and he was prepared for those kinds of thoughts, however nobody knew about his rather exceptional hearing but Lord Greis, and he thought they had done a good job of keeping it that way. Being special was rather frowned upon, and unfortunate accidents tended to happen to those who displayed excessive physical prowess. It was generally thought that humans had rather strict limitations, and anyone exceeding them had been tainted by a demon that was intent on destroying all humanity. Varan had his doubts about demonic corruption in general, and he was fairly sure that he himself had reached where he was through training, not any sort of supernatural influence, but one could never be sure. He remembered the thought that wasn't his own last night and internally shuddered.

"A spy? People commonly think that of me on first meeting, Sordrel, but I think you'll find I'm just a historian. I'm certainly interested in politics and current events, but I believe spying closes doors to you, all for the sake of money or power from some patron noble. It's a silly and dangerous game in my mind. I prefer my books, which are common knowledge to all." He paused a moment and eyed Sordrel critically. "Well to the literate anyway, though I suppose someone could read to those who aren't."

Sordrel gave Varan a knowing wink. "Sure, Varan. We have eyes to see, and ears to hear. You're not the only one with talents. In any case, dawn is truly breaking now, so I think this is a conversation to have another time. People will be waking up soon."

Varan wasn't quite sure what to think. Were these men truly supernatural in nature? Was that why they could fight off the guards so easily even unarmed? It was simpler to think that it was some conspiracy and that the guards were in on it, but was that truly the case? As Sordrel woke the rest of the refugees, and the group continued traveling toward Thorlin's Point, Varan thought on how he could get to the bottom of this mystery.

**

There was so much to do ever since Comanatin had begun his little revolution. Sveria hadn't been this busy since The Culling. It was nearing dusk, and she was in her room dressing like a servant in preparation to leave. The local nobles were well in hand now. The incursions by Comanatin's minions only served to help her cause with them. She would have her army. Now she needed to focus on tying up loose ends, and perhaps start working with the nobles in the other cities.

She finished her rather crude disguise with a cap to cover her long, blood red, hair. Anyone who knew her would recognize her instantly from her face and bearing, but that was irrelevant. She was trying to avoid irritating questions, and she'd found that the simplest of disguises worked best with humans. If you were feared enough they would simply pretend they had seen nothing rather than risk your wrath.

As she left her room she gave the guard a smile. "The lady is resting, Lor. She's not to be disturbed until I return."

Lor smiled and nodded.

"Off to run errands for Lady Cruor again? You've been busy lately. Never you worry, I'll keep her safe."

Sveria laughed as she continued downstairs and out the service entrance. It was something of a game she had with the servants to give character to her rather rudimentary disguise. Her servants were very carefully chosen, so she had no fears of them talking. Over the centuries she had groomed certain family lines into excellent servants. They would bleed for her, should it ever come to that.

Many servants were in the streets, either buying supplies before the shops closed, or walking home after a long day. The alley she was looking for was quite easy to spot by the void of people in its general vicinity. People made a deliberate effort to put as much space between them and that alley as possible, despite the fact that it was in a rather prosperous and safe area. Accidently stumbling into that alley was death, and everyone knew it. Sveria headed directly for it, to the shock of some of the people in the street.

At first glance, it appeared to be simply an empty alley, with no other exits. As Sveria focused her will, however, she easily saw through the illusions and walked up to one of the many doors that lined it, throwing it open.

Inside the building, she saw a blonde young man lounging on a sofa, eating some grapes, with a collection of sparsely clothed women fawning over him. Upon noticing the blood red hair on one of the women, Sveria grimaced.

"You go too far with your illusions, Relin."

A dagger appeared in her hand, and shot into the empty air to her left. A grunt came from that direction, and the women disappeared, though the man did not.

"You're getting better at concentration Relin, though your accuracy needs work. I have no blade tattoos, much less in the area your twisted mind seems to think. Are you ready to talk business or is that dagger in your stomach going to distract you?"

The blonde figure replied with casual indifference. "I can deal with it after you leave."

Sveria laughed. "You don't think I'm letting you keep the dagger do you? I'll be taking it with me when I go."

The figure scowled. "Of course you will be. What business do you have with me, Sveria? Is this a standard assassination or is this about our special arrangement?"

Sveria shook her head. "Neither. I'm not here to tell you to kill someone, quite the opposite. I want you to stay out of the situation with the revolutionaries."

The figure scoffed. "You know how I work. Do you really expect me to turn down the biggest contract in history just so you can play army?"

Sveria laughed. "How did your last big contract go, Relin? Do you still have that scar I gave you?"

The figure shrugged and gestured toward its face and body. "As you can plainly see, madam, I have no scars."

"Your illusion of course, has none. But then your illusion is a human, and has hair. Why are all of you elves bald anyway? You're not even that old. What are you, five hundred?"

"Seven. The baldness is because elven punishments are overly dramatic. What do you mean by all of us elves anyway? I'm the only elf in the human lands."

Sveria shrugged. "The instigator of this little revolution is an elf. He's a necromancer from before the time of The Culling, and not to be trifled with. I have enough on my plate without needing to deal with your reanimated corpse as well."

The figure smiled broadly. "A necromancer huh? What makes him so dangerous? The so called immortals he has as pets seem feeble enough, even if they are above your average person."

Sveria shook her head. "Comanatin is a being on a level that you are incapable of understanding, Relin. He and I both fought in The Culling, and while he is weak and pathetic compared to me, the fools you've killed in the past are nothing compared to his power. He would crush you as easily as I would, and then reanimate your corpse as a mindless abomination to decimate his enemies."

The figures smile grew even broader, and then disappeared to be replaced with another person entirely, still smiling. Relin was a short man, with a lean, wired build. His skin was so dark that it appeared to absorb light into it, which made it difficult to identify his exact features.

"Just how easily would you crush me, Sveria?"

Sveria looked over to the corner and noted that her dagger had passed harmlessly through the masked illusion she had thought was Relin.

"Clever, Relin, but I came here to talk, not kill you. You don't really think that would have fooled me in a fight, do you?"

Relin laughed darkly. "You wound me mistress, why ever would I want to fight you? I've always said that when the fight is joined, the battle is lost."

Sveria snorted in disgust. "Cute. Stay away from Comanatin if you value your life, Relin. I have things to do and can't afford to waste more time on you. If you think your silly illusory tricks give you a chance against veterans of The Culling, you have another thing coming."

Sveria turned to leave, her dagger floating from its

place on the floor back into her hand.

"Goodbye, Relin. I'll return as scheduled to give you more of the special targets."

"Farewell, Sveria. Have fun with your necromancer."

**

Varan wasn't sure what to make of the revolutionaries so far. Sordrel had said the other immortals moved on ahead during the night to help prepare for their arrival, and he had just laughed when Varan asked about the possibility of pursuit by the town guards. "The others would know in time to get back, don't worry about it."

Sordrel carried himself with an air of inevitable victory, and the refugees picked up on it. During the day Varan spoke with many of them, and found that they each had different ideas on how the revolution would succeed, but that they all shared Sordrel's belief that the nobility would be helpless to stop them. These same men who mere days before had been groveling for the scraps from the plates of nobility had apparently forgotten the power that had kept them down for so long. It was somewhat disconcerting to see. Were people's beliefs so easy to change? Did these people truly lose all their fear of the nobility overnight?

Varan also found that many of the refugees seemed to care more about the downfall of the nobles than their own freedom or livelihoods. Most seemed to have some sort of grievance with the nobles. Some had some ideal society they wanted to create, which usually differed from the society suggested by their peers. But many simply wanted the strength the immortals offered to have an outlet against the world at large. They wanted the power to harm those who had, in their minds, wronged them, and Varan got the distinct impression that many of these men would have joined the nobles in putting down this revolution if the immortals showed any sign of weakness or spurned their more sadistic outlets.

That night Varan went to talk to Sordrel, in the hopes of warning him of the danger these types of men could pose.

"They're just letting off some steam, Varan. They're good people at heart."

"I don't think you've heard the things these men are saying, Sordrel. One was saying that the first thing he'd do upon becoming an immortal was have his way with a noblewoman who once called him a petty thief."

Sordrel shook his head. "It's talk, Varan. It doesn't mean anything. You don't know how hard it is living in a world of nobles. How would you like to be called a thief?"

Varan laughed. "You mean when I was lying on the ground restrained by the guards after having stolen a woman's purse? He told the full story, Sordrel. He is a thief. Half the men here are criminals, and they seem proud of that fact."

Sordrel sighed. "Desperate times can drive men to desperate acts, Varan."

Varan shook his head. "I'm not talking about men who stole a loaf of bread to feed their families, Sordrel. How are you planning to keep these people under control if you train them to become like you?"

Sordrel shrugged. "When everyone is equal, there won't be a problem."

Varan pushed the issue. "And before then? When some are powerful and some are still weak and vulnerable? How long will it take to train the entire populace?"

Sordrel looked thoughtful. "A few generations most likely."

Varan was taken aback. "What?"

"It's not training, Varan. It's a procedure, and currently only one man can do it. It'll take time."

Varan was stunned. Sordrel had mentioned surgery before, but he hadn't taken him seriously. What was going on here? As he sat in silence, Sordrel continued.

"We're looking for leaders, Varan. The people who brought me into the immortals and trained me are too busy making new immortals to lead the revolution themselves, and I can't do everything on my own. Once we've taken cities we'll need people in charge to make sure they don't dissolve into chaos, but I need to move on to work on other cities. So we need leaders, and lots of them. That's the primary reason we're bringing people back to Thorlin's Point. I think you have promise, Varan. I know you work for Greis, and he's been good to you, but you need to think of the rest of humanity."

Varan wasn't sure what to say. "I'm a historian, not a leader."

Sordrel scoffed. "You can drop the act Varan. I know you're here to spy on us. We had a plant listening in on your conversation with Greis before you left."

Varan immediately thought about the crow he saw as he left the mansion, but that was impossible. "I don't know what you're talking about. In any case, I don't know the first thing about your organization, how can you expect me to be a leader in it?"

Sordrel nodded. "You're right. I'll explain how we work." He seemed to collect his thoughts for a moment. "As I said, I'm the leader of the immortals, but I'm not the founder. The founder is a man named Comanatin, and he's mastered immortality. Rather than keep the secret to himself, he's now spreading it to the rest of the world. Those of us who go through the procedure become like me, the immortals."

Varan gave Sordrel an odd look. "You literally believe you're immortal?"

Sordrel shook his head. "Not technically, but in the practical sense, yes. I'm near impossible to kill, and even if I die, Comanatin could still raise me from the dead so long as my brain wasn't too horribly damaged. The mind is the tricky part of reanimation or so I'm told. In any case, there's a woman named Sveria who controls mankind right now through her puppets, the nobility. She has her hand in everything, and she's the same woman you thought was responsible for our revolution. She goes by Lady Cruor."

Varan scoffed. "Are you seriously suggesting that Lady Cruor is the blood letter from the ancient myths?"

Sordrel nodded. "What's Lady Cruor's first name? When was she born? How has her family become so powerful with no apparent members?"

Varan shrugged. "The family is powerful enough that they can keep secrets quite well. It's pretty well known that she has trusted agents in every city, and it's assumed that the top ranking ones are members of the family. Nobody who tries to look into it too closely survives, so people have stopped looking. That isn't evidence of her being a legendary monster, however."

"Oh she's no monster. She's human. But she is the blood letter, and the only reason she's allowed us to collect recruits is she believes we're preparing for an all out war and that any recruits we have will just be blood sacks for her to fuel her magic with."

It took all of Varan's training and willpower not to laugh. "And why is Comanatin out to defeat her?"

"She would never allow the immortals to spread. Comanatin's goal is to eradicate death. Sveria is one of the largest bringers of death in the world. She delights in the slaughter, and the stability Comanatin would bring is anathema to her. She's also taken to having everyone that shows any strength of will murdered to reinforce the idea that humanity is weak and the supernatural is the exclusive domain of demons and monsters."

"And what proof do you have of all this, Sordrel? This is quite the story."

Sordrel laughed. "Well I could call some of the nearby familiars to join us if you want."

Suddenly, there was a small rush of wind, as if the air itself was being pushed out of the way and a robed figure stood beside Sordrel. A voice appeared in Varan's mind, though it seemed directed at Sordrel.

'I'll not have you wasting the time of my familiars on parlor tricks, Sordrel. I need to get back to the tower so I'll make this quick.'

The figure's voice continued, but it seemed now to be focusing directly on Varan.

'What Sordrel says is the truth, Varan. I could perform any number of magic tricks you want, but that would be a waste of

both of our time. I am Comanatin. You are a rational man, who lives in a very dull, scripted world, controlled by a woman by the name of Sveria. You have talents, and I think you're wise enough to know that you're not the only one. You have been lucky as of yet, that you have done an excellent job of hiding those talents. Sveria has you under watch, but has not decided to have you killed yet because you amuse her and she is not certain it's you with the abilities. You know of the suspicious deaths of those who show a bit too much potential, I am sure. It is your job to know such things. The evidence lies in front of you, Varan. See to it that you pay attention.'

With another rush of wind, the figure was gone. Varan wasn't entirely sure he had been there to begin with. He had seen enough strange things to take this seriously, however. He didn't necessarily trust Sordrel's version of events, but he would listen.

"So how did you get involved in all this, Sordrel?"

Sordrel smiled. "Let me tell you a story, Varan."

Sordrel told Varan the tale that I later transcribed into The Necromancer's Bargain. He began with the nightmares, and ended with the beginning of his will training.

"The will training hasn't gone so well, I'll admit. I haven't figured it out yet." He trailed off, and sat in silence as Varan contemplated what he'd just heard.

Sordrel appeared earnest, and his story didn't have any obvious holes in it. The mind control worried him somewhat, but the very fact that it worried him implied to him that it was either weak, as Comanatin said in the story, or didn't exist at all. He recalled his thought from the night before that didn't feel like his own, and wondered if that was the kind of impact the will had.

83

This Comanatin person worried Sordrel, however. If he was truly as powerful as he sounded he was incredibly dangerous, and he implied a level of mental domination over the immortals. How in control of himself was Sordrel? Was he even capable of thinking of the potential treachery Comanatin could commit once he had control of the human lands?

In Varan's experience, nobody was as benevolent as they appeared. As soon as a person got power, they tended to abuse it. There were the occasional exceptions, Lord Greis was quite powerful, but Varan had never seen him abuse that power to sadistic ends. But such exceptions were rare. Could humanity really risk allowing Comanatin free reign? By the sounds of it, he could murder everyone and turn them into undead slaves.

He was in a difficult situation. They were quite near the forest now, despite the slow time they made with the refugees in tow, and he was sure that Comanatin's minions would be able to track him down if he fled, but he knew that he couldn't continue forward to Thorlin's Point. If Comanatin could really do the things Sordrel said, then his very mind could be at stake.

"It's getting late, Sordrel. I need to sleep on this. It's a lot to think about all at once."

Sordrel nodded. "I could use some sleep too. I think it's been three days and I'm not thinking as clearly as I should be. I know it's a lot to take in, Varan, but consider my offer. It's for the good of humanity."

Varan nodded, and went to the edge of camp to lie down, listening to Sordrel's breathing as he went. He had a strong sounding set of lungs, and it was easy to make it out among all the snoring and breathing of the other members of the camp. Shortly after Sordrel's breathing leveled out into the steady rhythm of sleep, Varan got himself up and fled into the night.

His departure seemed to go unnoticed, but Varan still listened intently for any pursuit. Constantly looking over his shoulder would only slow him down. Within a few minutes, he heard the flapping of wings, and a large crow flew past him, to land a few feet in front, seeming to be keeping a safe distance. Varan heard the same voice in his head that had come from the figure previously, this time seeming to come from the crow.

'Sordrel will be displeased that you didn't at least say farewell, Varan. He likes you.'

Varan walked around the crow. "I'm sorry to disappoint, but I'm not slowing down so pursuit can catch me."

After passing the crow, he broke into a run, hoping to get more distance from the camp before more pursuers arrived. The crow flew above his head, and the voice continued.

'There's no need for such a rush, Varan. I have no intention of sending anyone to pursue you. Sordrel is getting some much needed sleep, and I have no interest in forcing you into anything. Of course if you were going to believe me you wouldn't have run off to begin with, and you're smart enough that I doubt you'll waste the breath you need for running to respond, so I will talk and you will just have to listen.'

Varan kept running, a bit surprised at the man's insight, but knew that responding would slow him down in the long run, and he would need every bit of speed he could get if he hoped to escape.

'We need leaders, as I said. You would have made an

excellent leader, and it's unfortunate that you've chosen to flee instead. Is it Sordrel's powers of the mind that frighten you? Or is it me? Whatever the reason, I understand this transition is difficult, and I'll give you your space to think, and observe. The world is about to change, Varan. Humanity lives in a paradise, yet it squanders the precious gift of safety on petty rivalries. This will not continue. Sveria has had her time of dominion, setting humanity at its own throat in a petty and continuous vengeance for the deeds of men long dead. But even for her villainy, she has protected humanity from the creatures that would destroy it entirely. You have no idea the creatures that live outside of this little piece of paradise that was created through the blood and sweat of the betrayed. But that time is done. I will give humanity the power to defend itself, and I will guide it not from the shadows as she does, but in the open, showing humanity the way to peace and prosperity. I bid you farewell for now, Varan. Know that I harbor no ill will for you. Given time I trust you will come to see things my way.'

The crow flew off, and the voice remained silent. Varan for a moment wondered if the voice was actually tied to an individual, or if it truly was inside his head, and there was no escape from it. The voice sounded benevolent enough, but he still had no trust for it. As he continued running, he thought about how to deal with powers such as these. If Sveria was truly human, and the suspicious deaths of the talented few truly were the assassinations of those with budding supernatural capabilities, she clearly needed to die. But if she were to die, Comanatin would be able to conquer all of humanity, and his power to create loyal servants that were leagues ahead of any other human would allow him to do whatever he wanted. How can you combat someone if all the powerful fighters belong to him?

If humanity was going to prosper, it needed to be out from under the thumb of these powerful few. The nobility kept each other in line to a point. The fear of other nobles prevented them from overextending themselves in their conflicts with each other, and thus kept competition mostly civil, and prevented the deaths and suffering of war. But with only two nobles, the system would collapse into a giant war, until one emerged as dictator.

The southern city of Passwatch seemed to run quite well without nobles, but thinking of a society without nobles was pointless. It was a pipe dream to think of eliminating the nobility entirely, unless he could get the total backing of Relin. Relin...Varan picked up the pace, heading for Thelryn, and the assassins he would need to carry out his desperate plan.

**

Upon his arrival in Thelryn, Varan was told by a servant that Lady Cruor had requested his presence two days prior. Keeping a powerful noblewoman waiting that long was almost unheard of, but his staff had told her messenger that he was bedridden with illness and would come as soon as he was able. It was early morning, and he certainly looked haggard enough to look the part after spending most of the night running without sleep. He decided he would meet Lady Cruor after securing Relin's services. If he died before enacting his plan, he worried that humanity was doomed.

Varan disguised himself as a servant, and went to find Relin. Finding Relin was never a difficult task. The group made no secret of their lair, and anyone who worked for high ranking nobility knew how to find them in the case of desperation. Desperation was required for someone to even consider hiring Relin. If the target wasn't deemed worthy of their time, or the person doing the hiring wasn't wealthy enough to afford it, the lives of both the messenger and the patron who sent them were forfeit.

Varan was desperate, however. Relin was the best, and by such a large margin that no other group compared. Nobody had ever caught a Relin assassin, and there was no record of a failed assassination that could be credibly tied to the group. Varan even had the suspicion that they could be the ones responsible for wiping out the supernatural population, as the only evidence of foul play was the general trend for talented people to die young rather than any evidence in the individual cases.

As he entered their alley, he was surprised to find a man standing there, waiting for him, though he was certain the man had not been there before he entered. He had heard no sounds indicating the man's movement, and Varan immediately suspected supernatural forces at work. The man was dressed richly, but practically. The kind of clothes a nobleman might wear when out on the town. He made no movement to speak or address Varan, and simply stood there with a disapproving scowl on his lips. Varan bowed deeply, and spoke.

"Greetings, sir. I apologize for bothering you so early in the morn, however I have business to discuss."

The man nodded slowly. "What kind of business draws the head spy of Lord Greis's household to our group?"

It didn't surprise Varan in the least that the man

knew his station. Everyone seemed to these days, and it was Relin's business to know everything about everyone. "I have two separate targets that need to be eliminated, with the priority being the first."

The man nodded again. "And these targets are?"

"The first target is a man or monster named Comanatin. He is the ringleader of the revolutionary organization known as the Immortals. I believe he makes his encampment in or near Thorlin's Point, but I'm afraid I don't have precise information on his location."

The man frowned. "We require rather precise identification before we take on a job. We refuse on principle any job where the target is not clearly identified, as killing the wrong target is bad for business."

Varan nodded. "That's understandable sir, but I think identifying Comanatin will not be hard. He has a host of supernatural abilities, including but not necessarily limited to speaking and seeing through the eyes of birds, teleportation, and the reanimation of the dead. I unfortunately can tell you little about his physical characteristics as he was wearing a dark robe and it was night time. He was of above average height, and had a lean build. He also made mention of a tower in my conversation with him."

The man nodded. "That should be sufficient identification for our purposes. You seem rather comfortable speaking of magic, sir. Do you have no fear that we'll simply scoff at your idle fancies and kill you for wasting our time?"

Varan shook his head. "There is no way you could have appeared so suddenly in this alley without my hearing it, except through supernatural means. I am confident that your organization is involved in the conspiracy that prevents the public from knowing about the supernatural, and that is part of why I came to your group. You should have experience dealing with people like Comanatin."

The man smiled strangely. "If we are part of the conspiracy, is it not dangerous to admit knowledge of it to us?"

Varan shrugged. "There are no safe ways to handle this situation, sir. I'm simply doing my best to ensure humanity has a future."

The man nodded, seemingly amused. "The price will be expensive, but a man like Lord Greis has sufficient funds to cover it. Who is the other target?"

Varan tried to maintain his cool. He was taking an extreme risk here. Relin was very likely involved with Lady Cruor in some way, and depending on how strong their business relationship was this could result in Varan's death.

He spoke firmly, and with conviction. "The other target is Lady Sveria Cruor."

The figure paused a moment. "That is not a name to be given lightly. We will have to consider whether even Lord Greis can afford two targets of this magnitude in one transaction."

Varan nodded. "Take the time you need, however keep in mind that with a power player like Lady Cruor gone, Greis will be in a position to dramatically increase his wealth, particularly with advanced knowledge."

The figure nodded. "This is true; however I refuse to work with theoretical futures. Lord Greis could die suddenly tomorrow and his inheritor could be incompetent. Regardless, I believe we shall accept both contracts, if only to see how you intend to fill the void of power that it will cause. Payment shall be taken at our leisure, and a receipt of payment shall be delivered to Lord Greis's bedchambers at a time when he is alone."

Varan bowed deeply. "Thank you, and your organization, for your service, sir."

The figure disappeared, as if he'd never been there, and a voice came in on the wind. "The pleasure is mine, Varan."

Meeting Lady Cruor was another risk, but not meeting her would be suicide. The only reason she would call someone like Varan for an audience was to check if he had skipped town, and Varan's late response would be proof enough that he had. The illness excuse was sufficient for both parties to save face, but Lady Cruor would certainly know he had left, and most likely have figured out why. Not showing up would immediately make him seem like a rebel sympathiser, which was the last thing he needed.

After returning to the house to change into proper clothes, Varan did his best to make himself look presentable, though the dark circles under his eyes from exhaustion certainly didn't help. He supposed they would at least corroborate the case that he had been ill rather than out and about.

After arriving at the Cruor household, one of the servants told Varan he would have to wait.

"We're terribly sorry but you've come at a busy time, if you could simply wait in the lounge she'll meet with you shortly."

Varan was content to wait. He had never been in the Cruor household before, and it was truly a sight to behold. There was a seemingly endless stream of messengers coming in the door, explaining something in code to one of the servants, and then leaving. As Varan listened more carefully to the conversations around the house from his place in the foyer, he noted that everyone, even the cooks seemed to be speaking in some sort of code to one another. The servants, for their part, seemed to be of a higher grade than most. They seemed to work continuously, and while they spoke to each other in a code Varan could not understand, they did not stop working to do so as was so common among servants.

Varan could make out no coherent dialogue during his wait, and he wondered whether perhaps that was due to his presence. He certainly did not go unnoticed. Everyone in the house seemed to be part of a singular unit, with him being the only outlier. The messengers always provided at least a cursory glance, and some smiled at him before making their report. He always smiled back, but their smiles felt like an adult smiling down at a child. It made him uncomfortable. Eventually he closed his eyes and simply focused on listening to the unfamiliar code, trying to figure it out before his audience with Lady Cruor.

His grogginess made it difficult to focus, and so he made little in the way of progress. He thought he had worked out the references to himself in the dialogue when a man spoke to him, and he opened his eyes.

"Lady Cruor will see you now."

Varan nodded, and followed the servant into a room that had a single door guard stationed outside.

Varan had seen Lady Cruor before, but he was always surprised by what a beautiful woman she was. She was, by anyone's standards, an old woman, but she looked no older than thirty years. Her hair was a vibrant red today, though he recalled it being a light pink the last time he had seen her, and he wondered if she used some sort of dye. Her skin was flawless, and had none of the signs of the heavy makeup that most noblewomen wore to hide their faults. She wore no jewelry, and her dress was rather simple, but perfectly designed to accentuate body, and the overall effect was amazing. Whereas most noblewomen seemed to scream "I am a noble! Look at me!" with their fashion, Lady Cruor made herself look to be an immaculate beauty. It was, Varan thought, an interesting strategy, and it made the other nobles seem somewhat childish in comparison.

She smiled warmly at him as he entered. "So I see you've finally decided to join me, Varan. Was your trip to see Relin profitable?"

Varan glanced at the door. The guard outside would be able to clearly hear anything said in the room. He didn't know how she had identified his trip to Relin, but speaking openly about Relin in earshot of a third party seemed foolish. Lady Cruor noticed his glance and spoke. "Looking to escape already?"

As he began to respond, she laughed and continued. "I'm just teasing. If I could not trust Lor, he would not be my door guard. I do not allow those I don't trust to work in my home."

Varan nodded. She seemed too light-hearted to know who he had hired Relin for, so he decided to go with partial honesty and hope for the best. "It was, milady. I tracked down the leader of the revolution, and Relin should deal with the problem expediently. They're a dangerous cult with a fanatic leading them named Sordrel.

He reports to a man that he treats as a sort of god, known as Comanatin. I felt it simplest to have both of them eliminated. Relin agreed to accept the contract."

Lady Cruor's eyebrow rose questioningly. "He accepted a contract on Comanatin?"

Varan nodded, and noting her usage of the singular form, followed suit. "He did, quite readily. I had to give him some identifying features, but otherwise he had no complaints. Is there a problem milady?"

Lady Cruor scowled. "That fool. I'll need to move quickly if I'm going to salvage this situation." She rose her voice toward the door. "Lor, go get Ulren. I need to send another message to the Pleir household."

As she idly returned her gaze to Varan he could see that he was merely an afterthought. She was already miles away, focusing on whatever she had planned. "Thank you for your report, Varan. If I have further need, I'll call upon you."

Varan bowed deeply. "I am at your service milady; however I will be leaving today to report back to my Lord. You shall be able to reach me there should you need me."

Lady Cruor nodded absently. "Of course. Goodbye Varan."

Varan bowed again, and let himself out. As he left Lady Cruor's home, he breathed a sigh of relief in knowing that the hard part was over. If Relin succeeded this nightmare would be over, but if they failed Varan wasn't sure how humanity could combat these titans. As he began the journey home, he tried to force his tired mind to formulate a plan.

**

The study was pitch black. The door stood open to the hall, but no draft or light issued from it.   There were no windows to let in light, as the sole occupant had no need or desire for any. The occupant was a tall man, with his leanly muscled build completely masked by the illusory black robe that covered his body, not allowing an inch of his telltale obsidian skin show. A quick glance at the man's angular face and sharp ears would indicate his elven nature. His obsidian skin identified him as an exile. He was busying himself mixing vials of chemicals together in a large beaker. He worked fluidly and precisely in the absolute darkness, his eyes seeing without the need for light. As he worked, he would adjust the temperature, or more accurately the energy, of both the vials themselves and the beaker with his will, ensuring the chemicals bonded in precisely the manner he desired.

As the figure worked, another figure entered the room. Beneath the masking illusions that completely hid his presence from prying eyes was another elf, somewhat shorter than the occupant of the room, with a similarly wired frame. This new figure held a long dagger at the ready as he slowly approached what he thought to be his unsuspecting victim.

'I see you've decided to finally make your move, Relin.'

The thought quite clearly came from the man at the table, and Relin , seeing his cover blown, raced to stab the figure with inhuman speed. In that instant the occupant of the room rose, turned and, still holding one of the vials, grabbed Relin by the wrist with his free hand, stopping the dagger a fraction of an inch from his chest. Relin, recognizing the figure's overpowering strength immediately, drew another dagger from his clothes and threw it at the man's chest, hoping to take him by surprise. He was doubly shocked as the figure let go of the vial he was holding, which remained suspended, and caught the dagger out of the air. Relin then suddenly and quite unexpectedly found himself unable to move, locked in place.

'You cannot win as you are, Relin. There is no mortal man on this plane who could defend himself against you, but you have overstepped the boundaries of your own mortal shell. You are an excellent specimen. You have trained your body and mind to their limits. Your illusions display a creativity and skill that is remarkable, and your strength and speed are magnificent. But you are still mortal, and have failed to take full advantage of your potential. You have two options today. The first is to continue as you are, the mortal assassin Relin Darkblade. So long as you leave these lands you need never encounter me ever again.'

The figure paused a moment.

'Your other option, I think, is more appealing to us both. I can improve your body and train your mind in ways you would never imagine possible. Between your skills and my enhancements, there will be none who can stand against you. Join with me, and you will taste power beyond your wildest dreams.'

Relin paused for a few moments, taking it all in, before a smile spread to his lips. On that night a shadow known to a select few as Sorelin, was born. The birth of Sorelin would herald in a new stage in the conflict, and the lands of men would never be the same.

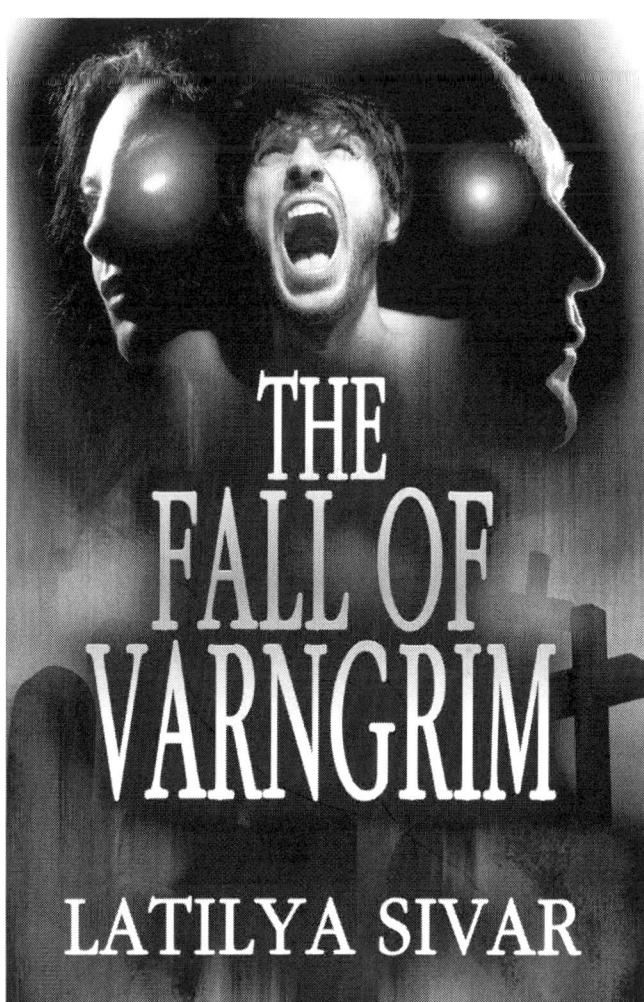

THE
FALL OF
VARNGRIM

LATILYA SIVAR

It may come as a surprise to many that this account of the War of the Dead has been completed, given the deceased status of our former narrator. However he was not the only man with an interest in seeing this history published in its entirety. For those who are unaware, Volrin Dahl, the narrator and primary contributor to "The Necromancer's Bargain" and "The Immortal Revolution." was executed in Midgar for treason some weeks ago. Apparently his claim that the hero Varan was the source for his "vile propaganda" was too much for certain people of power to tolerate.

I helped Volrin to edit his stories, and I added a few pieces of my own to the bargain as well. Varan obviously had no knowledge of Comanatin's talks with Gingko, for instance, and thus could not have left them in his notes. I, as most readers know, have my own sources. This is the continuation and conclusion of "The War of the Dead". It is dedicated to Volrin Dahl, who did not live to see the completion of his work, and if the powers that be have an interest in punishing me for completing this history, they can certainly try.

But enough about current events, sad as they may be. This is a story about the war that is responsible for Midgar as we know it, and the people who made it happen. Volrin's records were destroyed when he was arrested, so I am forced to draw upon my own resources. I shall focus on some of the key moments among the power players of the time, but I will also attempt to bring home some of the impact these events had on the pawns.

We begin with one such pawn named Arden, a young man who answered Lady Cruor's call to arms, hoping to defend his city from whatever was responsible for the insurrection in Thorlin's Point.

**

Arden found himself once again wishing he were back home in Thelryn. He had joined the militia Lady Cruor had raised, only to find himself trapped in a nightmare. He was sure that this forsaken forest would be the doom of them all, and though it was not his turn on watch, he found himself listening for the shouts and screams that would herald the return of the walking dead.

The journey from Thelryn to Thorlin's Point had started smoothly. As they headed north across the open fields, there were no hints of resistance from their supposed enemies. It wasn't until they arrived at the edge of the forest that things began to change. They had been met at the edge of the forest by a lone man. When he spoke, his voice seemed to speak straight to the mind itself.

'You are now entering the lands of the Immortals, at the behest of an enemy of the people. Know that should you enter this forest with evil intent, you shall never leave.'

The soldiers had laughed at that, and one man went so far as to shoot an arrow at the distant figure, who promptly vanished into thin air. This made some of the soldiers uncomfortable, but the laughter at the "fleeing wretch" was contagious, and nobody thought long on it.

The soldiers made good time on the first day, following the road toward Thelcrest. The plan had been to analyze the situation in Thelcrest, before moving on to Thorlin's Point, where the cult was stationed. It was that night that everything changed.

As the soldiers sat around the campfire, eating and boasting of how they would crush the traitors that were trying to destroy society, a fel wind came upon them, and their fires extinguished, leaving them in darkness. It was then that the dead came upon them, wielding clubs with inhuman strength. The creatures were seemingly invulnerable. The swords the soldiers sliced into dead flesh, but the damage was cosmetic, the dead cared not for their wounds. After battle was joined, however, the Lady Cruor revealed herself from among the soldiers, and with a strength and ferocity that seemed inhuman, she cleaved flesh and bone alike, tearing the dead asunder with her might. As the battle began to turn, the dead simply vanished, leaving the wounded soldiers as the only evidence they had ever been there at all.

The sun never came up that morning, and the forest itself conspired to seal their doom. The path ended a short distance from where they rested, and they soon found themselves hopelessly lost. Having to carry the wounded slowed them down even further, but it seemed not to matter.

No matter how far they travelled it was trees as far as the eye could see. The Lady Cruor tried to lead them, but whenever she would lead in the direction she claimed held the road, she would simply disappear. Sometimes she would be gone for seconds, sometimes for hours at a time, after which she would curse their incompetence and weak wills.

The dead came whenever the soldiers settled to rest, and any who strayed far from the group disappeared into the forest, never to return. Their numbers were dwindling, and now they had more wounded than healthy. With no way to move so many injured, the group had stopped completely, and now they awaited the next coming of the dead.

Lady Cruor was sitting by herself at the edge of camp, seemingly deep in thought. As Arden watched her, he felt himself calm. The dead were proving to be a horrific foe, but Lady Cruor mowed them down like blades of grass, and no soldiers had yet died in battle thanks to her heroics. As he thought on this, she stood up and walked over to the wounded soldiers, eying them thoughtfully. Arden hoped she was coming up with a plan to get them all home. She nodded to herself, apparently coming to a decision.

Suddenly, there came a shout from the other end of the camp and Arden looked back to see a swarm of the dead that had appeared amongst the soldiers. As he stood and prepared for battle once again, he glanced toward the wounded soldiers, expecting to see Lady Cruor charging into battle.

She was gone. Arden tried to convince himself that he had simply missed her, and that she would join the battle momentarily, but as he faced the coming tide of the dead, his hope shattered, and as he rose his sword feebly against the cadaver that stood before him, another snuck through his defenses from the side, and he fell into darkness.

**

Sveria rushed through the forest, the dead weight of the unconscious soldier on her back not slowing her in the slightest. Between the illusions created by Relin, and Comanatin's shamblers, the soldiers were mostly useless, but if she was going to defeat Comanatin she would need blood to fuel her magic.

Relin had managed to lead the group far astray. Despite her attempts to lead them, the fools seemed unable to move closer to either Thorlin's Point or Thelcrest. She had caught the occasional glimpse of Relin, but he kept himself too far away to safely intercept.

Now she was running for Thorlin's Point. It was further than Thelcrest, but she anticipated that Comanatin would have evacuated Thelcrest due to its close proximity to the edge of the forest. There was no reason to waste time on an empty village. Making a move on Thorlin's Point would force Comanatin to act. He couldn't retreat indefinitely.

As she ran, an explosive burst of wind signaled Comanatin teleporting a group of shamblers into her path. Sveria unceremoniously dumped the soldier onto the ground, where he groaned and shifted, apparently beginning to come to his senses. She didn't have to worry about him fleeing, however. His legs had been broken by the undead.

Drawing her sword, Sveria cut a thin line down the leg of the soldier, and began searching the area with her will for Comanatin, as the undead descended upon her. The necromancer had clearly been trying to draw her away from her fuel source; otherwise he would have teleported the shamblers in practically on top of her rather than at a distance. She stood astride the fallen soldier as she cleaved heads and limbs from the shamblers that came within her reach. Eventually they stopped, but Sveria could feel a far larger group approaching through the forest, and heard Comanatin's voice on the wind.

"Why do you insist on fighting me, Sveria? You've grown soft over the centuries, and stand no chance of killing me. Even at your full power, you could not destroy me. What do you hope to accomplish while you are weak from centuries of inactivity?"

Sveria spat at the ground, narrowly missing the soldier whose eyes were open now, glancing between the forest and Sveria, terrified.

"Your shamblers stand no chance against me, Comanatin. Your magic can't harm me, and your combat capabilities are nothing compared to mine. I think it is you that is in the hopeless situation, not me."

The voice laughed. "While all of those things are true, Sveria. It is also true that without blood to fuel you, my shamblers and I are, in fact, a match for you in the melee, and that while you have no need for sleep, you will certainly need to drink eventually. You cannot stand on your blood sack forever. I can simply wait until desperation forces you to find water, though I imagine by that time your friend would be long dead from dehydration and no longer suitable for your needs.

Sveria scowled, and looked down at the soldier beneath her. "We need to get moving. Thorlin's Point is close, and if we can reach it, we can destroy the necromancer."

The soldier looked down at his useless legs, before looking back to her and asking the question that had hounded him since his awakening. "Where are the others? Are we the only survivors?"

Sveria shook her head. "They're fighting, and they're counting on us to destroy this creature before they're overwhelmed."

The voice laughed. "Sveria abandoned them to die when she realized she couldn't carry more than one of you without encumbering herself, and the others would never be able to reach me. Luckily for them, I have no intention of killing any of you. They are being healed by an associate of mine as we speak."

Sveria snarled. "He lies! I will not stand here and listen to this. We're going, Veridin."

With that, she grabbed Veridin and slung him across her shoulder like a sack of potatoes, before charging forward to cut a path through the shamblers. As she reached them, however, she felt a telltale rush of wind behind her, and ducked suddenly to avoid the kick that came toward her head, dropping Veridin again in the process, who hit the ground with a pained yelp. As she turned to face Comanatin, another rush of wind heralded his disappearance, and she cursed angrily. Suddenly, a rush of wind came from all around her, but it had the distinct feeling of one of Relin's illusions. Not knowing where the attack was coming from, she ducked to the ground, and sliced another cut into the poor soldier that had the misfortune of being chosen by her. As she did so, the kick landed, but focusing her will she enhanced her reflexes, grabbing hold of the foot as it made contact, only to have it dissipate into nothing with a rush of wind.

Veridin was crying now, both in pain from his wounds, and terror that the woman he had thought of as a savior was cutting slices into his flesh. As Sveria began fighting off another wave of shamblers above him, Veridin felt a strange sensation in his legs, and with an odd crack, the pain from both the cuts and the breaks disappeared. He tried moving his legs slightly, and realized they were no longer broken. As he was about to stand to bolt into a run, a voice materialized in his head.

'Not yet.'

Too frightened to disobey, he remained still as Sveria finished with the shamblers.

"Is that all you have, Comanatin? Next time I catch that foot of yours, it will be with my sword, not my hand."

The only response was a sudden rush of wind, and four robed figures appeared on each side of her, readying kicks.

'Now, Veridin!'

Veridin bolted, looking back only long enough to see the figures dissipate as if they hadn't been there at all, and Sveria's snarl of rage as she turned toward him to follow. He turned forward again and focused all his effort into escaping without tripping over the roots and undergrowth that made up the floor of the forest. There was a distinct clash of steel as Sveria became embroiled in another fight, but over time the sounds grew distant and eventually dissipated entirely.

**

Sordrel was walking through the streets of Thelryn. It felt strange to see guards and have them smile at him, or deliver status reports. He had so recently been fighting or fleeing from some of these same men. Once Sorelin got involved things had started moving faster, and Sordrel wasn't entirely certain that he liked it.

They had stopped recruiting people away to Thorlin's Point. There was no point now that Comanatin wasn't there. Sortira was holding down the fort so to speak, but since the takeovers of Ilar and Thelryn, the core of the revolution had moved down to Thelryn to be closer to the front lines.

The takeovers had gone smoothly. Sorelin would sneak into the city in advance, and kidnap all of the most powerful nobles to create a power vacuum. Sordrel and the rest of the Immortals would come in once the vacuum had destabilized the city, and reinstitute order. The people's fear of the nobles dissipated readily, and they supported the takeover with great zeal.

The nobles that remained fought the change of course, but their guards and servants simply weren't loyal enough to fight for them. The nobles fought with words and calls for violence, but they were mostly drowned out by the voices of the rest of the people, eager to throw off their tyranny.

There was occasional fighting, mostly breaking up riots since the most powerful nobles were out of the picture, and thus unable to organize their guards. The remaining nobles were quick to try and usurp the positions of the powerful, and their internal bickering helped further fracture their already divided faction. The one exception was the Cruor household in Thelryn. No nobles remained in the home with Sveria fleeing through the eastern countryside from Comanatin, but the guards and servants fought rabidly to defend their master's residence. Sordrel was shocked to find such fervent loyalty to someone as vicious and cruel as Sveria. After having to violently subdue every member of the household to confiscate their weapons, Sordrel tried to convince them to reintegrate with the rest of the city, but the household continued their underground resistance despite the lack of popular support.

Sordrel sighed as he imagined them trying to get arms from the black market in preparation for Sveria's return. They had an unwavering devotion to Sveria, and seemed to think she was the driving force of human progress. Without her, humanity was doomed in their minds. It was going to be a long road getting them back on track, and the Immortals would have to be very careful to maintain their public image with the Cruor household waiting for their chance to strike.

Despite the problems with Sveria's legacy, the conquests felt like liberation more so than annexation, but Sordrel's will still bothered him. He had made some progress in understanding it, but he still worried that his will was controlling people, and that the revolution wouldn't truly be one of the people until he could stop its subtle manipulations.

His thoughts were interrupted by Sortira asking him a question from back in Thorlin's Point.

'How are things going in Thelryn, Sordrel?'

'Smoothly, same as Ilar. Most of those who would resist simply fled, a lot of nobles are gathering in Varngrim right now, I'd wager.'

'How is your training coming along?'

'Slowly, Sortira. You know that. I think I'll be able to control it before reaching Varngrim, though. I'm starting to get a handle on it.'

'Are you still planning to stop using your will once you gain control over it?'

'Yes. I know you and Comanatin don't approve, but if we're in the right, I see no reason to deprive people of their freedom of choice.'

'It isn't mind control, you know. It's more like steering people toward an appropriate response.'

'I don't want to hear it. This is a revolution of the people, and I don't want to override their voices with my own.'

'If you say so, Sordrel, but revolution is not normally such a clean business.'

'How would you know? Nobody has ever led a successful revolt before.'

'Comanatin has told me stories... In any case, be careful Sordrel, and if things start to go badly make sure you use all options available to you.'

'We'll see.'

**

Varan felt helpless. Relin had clearly failed, and rather spectacularly at that. Lady Cruor had formed an army that marched on Thorlin's Point, but never returned, and now the Immortals had taken Ilar and Thelryn.

Refugees had been streaming into Varngrim for days now, mostly minor nobles and their personal guards. It seemed that before the conquest of the cities, the Immortals had eliminated the leadership. All the most influential and powerful nobles, whose guards kept law and order within the city, disappeared overnight. In the ensuing chaos, the Immortals would simply walk in the front gates, and claim ownership of the city. Varan suspected Relin's involvement in the disappearances. The disappearances were just too perfectly orchestrated to be anyone else. No trace of the victims was ever found.

The nobles were stripped of their titles, and their homes were being used as shelters for the poor. There had been skirmishes between the Immortals and some of the more loyal guards, but most simply abandoned their posts rather than face the powerful invaders. The Immortals didn't seem to be locking down the city, and so most of the nobility took their more loyal servants and fled to Varngrim.

Varngrim itself wasn't faring very well. The merchants didn't seem to particularly care about the revolution. With the Immortals leaving the gates open it didn't impede their trade at all, and as the nobles started locking themselves in their homes, they were stocking up on supplies in case of a siege. The nobles and their servants were struggling, however. The stream of noble refugees from Ilar and Thelryn was dramatically increasing demand for some of the finer things in life, and the servants they brought with them needed to eat. Prices were skyrocketing already, and it had only been a few days. It was a wonderful time to be a merchant, but the situation was deteriorating rapidly for everyone else.

As Varan thought on this, a guard approached him. Varan recognized him as one of the three men stationed to Lord Greis's study. The man approached with a sickened look, before whispering the words Varan had been dreading since this whole thing began.

"Lord Greis is gone."

**

As Sordrel gazed upon the walls of the city of Varngrim, he frowned at the reports he was getting from the crows. Shortly after Varan's return to Varngrim, Comanatin's crow familiars found themselves the targets of a bounty, originating from the Greis household. They hadn't been able to land, or even fly low, near the city ever since. Because of this the reports lacked detail, and Sorelin had already moved on to aid Comanatin with Sveria. Despite the lack of detail, however, things were clearly not going as planned.

In the first few hours, the city had shown some of the same signs of instability as Ilar and Thelryn, however, a large group of soldiers from the Greis household had gone through the city, and appeared to absorb the soldiers working for the other disappearing nobles as they instituted martial law. The citizens were mostly contained to their homes, and the guards patrolling the streets prevented any sort of unified resistance. In short, where they had expected riots, they had instead found military order and discipline. This was going to be a tough nut to crack.

It was tempting to continue waiting, but any revolt at this point would be a frightening thing. Starved, caged, people lashing out at their captors. In the previous cities, soldiers were as much a part of the rebellion as the peasantry, and the resulting confusion prevented any sort of unified resistance. Order disintegrated far before it reached the point of mass violence. Here though, with such rigid control, it would begin with violence, a spark that could create an inferno. They would need to act before it reached that point if they wanted to avoid deaths in the ensuing chaos.

Lord Greis and Varan were clearly responsible for the order. Everything centered on the Lord's mansion, despite Sorelin removing Greis himself from the picture. The man had clearly set up procedures in case of his disappearance, but if the center of control were taken completely, Sordrel figured this city would join as willingly if not more so than Ilar and Thelryn had. There would be no need to use his will if they took the city cleanly.

The Immortals would go in first, followed by soldiers that had joined them thus far. Some came from the troops that had originally assaulted Thorlin's Point, others had joined them in the cities, and still others were volunteers from the peasantry, outfitted with equipment taken from the soldiers who refused to join their ranks. They were there to keep order, not fight the enemy directly.

After a final check of the soldiers, Sordrel gave the Immortals the signal to charge.

The soldiers on the wall reacted instantly to the

Immortal charge, and when they were within range of their bows Sordrel bristled as the first volley flew toward them. He knew logically that the arrows were no threat, but on an instinctual level, it was terrifying to charge directly into the line of fire. As the first volley flew overhead, the archers having underestimated the speed at which the Immortals moved, Sordrel picked up the pace.

Another volley, this time closer, and another that fell directly on the group of Immortals. Sordrel dodged out of the way as an arrow came directly at him, then before the archers could reload to fire another time, he was bounding up the wall, the rough stone giving plenty of purchase for his strong, callused hands.

As Sordrel reached the top, he was greeted by a trio of halberds stabbing toward him. With a final leap, Sordrel flipped over the weapons, and as the guards tried to recover for another swing, got in beneath the first soldier's guard and tore the halberd from his grip.

The rest of the Immortals were on the wall now, facing off with other guards. As the two remaining guards stabbed toward Sordrel, another Immortal, Oberon, came up from behind, and with a quick sweep, took down the first, before striking behind the other guard's knee, dislocating the bone and causing him to crumple instantly. Sordrel nodded toward Oberon, and after tossing the halberds over the wall, descended the stairs to street level, where they met more resistance.

The gate was guarded by four men, armed with the same halberds that were so popular among noble guards. The men immediately charged Sordrel, two stabbing toward him with the spear end of the halberd, as the other two attempted to flank him. Sordrel dodged to the left, and the soldier there tried to slice into him with the axe head, only to be stopped short as Sordrel grabbed the shaft just under the head, and tore it from the man's hands.

Oberon came in from the other side, and as Sordrel tripped the man he had just disarmed, Oberon took down the man on the right with a kick that sent him sprawling to the ground. Sordrel tossed the halberd onto a roof to get it out of the way. Nodding to each other, the two Immortals advanced upon the remaining two guards, who tried to keep them at bay with the sharp spearheads of their weapons.

Moving in synch, the two Immortals dodged to either side, and moving faster than the men could react, grabbed their weapons, tore them from their hands, and tripped them with them.

As the rest of the Immortals began coming down from the wall, Sordrel ran over to the gate, and, tossing the enormous wooden bar out of the way as if it were a twig, pulled it open to let in the rest of the soldiers.

Sordrel took a mental inventory of the state of the battle. All of the Immortals were now with him in front of the gate, with the wall guards incapacitated and disarmed. The crows were reporting that more guards were heading their way, alerted by the commotion on the walls. It seemed that most of the guards in the city were heading toward their way, with only small numbers remaining on their patrol routes to keep the populace in their homes.

As the soldiers began heading toward the city, Sordrel addressed the Immortals. "Most of the guards are heading this way. The crows should keep you informed of their locations. Oberon, you're with me. The rest of you, wait for the others to arrive, then start fanning out. I want the city under control as quickly as possible. If the civilians start thinking we need help, they'll just get themselves hurt."

Sordrel nodded to Oberon, and the two began running toward the Greis household, near the center of the city. The sight of the crows supplied Sordrel with a detailed overhead map as they dodged into back alleys to avoid incoming guards. They didn't want to cause a ruckus in the middle of town and get bogged down before reaching their destination. The rest of the Immortals would deal with the guards.

It took awhile to reach the Greis household, but it went without incident thanks to the crows. In addition to the fighting near the gate, there was some sort of disturbance a short way north of their destination. They would need to hurry.

The Greis household appeared to have only a skeleton crew guarding the courtyard. There weren't enough guards that had remained loyal to keep the peace in the city while simultaneously guarding its key points, and whoever was in charge had clearly decided to emphasize riot control rather than their own defense. Sordrel had his ideas of who was behind it, but the leader hadn't come out of the mansion, so he couldn't be positive. As he and Oberon stood in an alley between the courtyard wall and a nearby building, he asked the crows for an update on the situation.

Of the ten guards in the courtyard, four of them were guarding the gate itself, two appeared to be messengers that had come from the north, near the disturbance, and the rest were patrolling the area in groups of two. They couldn't be sure how many guards were inside the building, but the other Immortals would have their hands tied, and he needed to secure a surrender before the situation to the north got out of control.

Sordrel nodded to Oberon, and the two men quickly scaled the courtyard wall, landing at a dead run toward the nearest patrolmen, who were taken completely by surprise. In near unison, Oberon and Sordrel grabbed the halberds of their respective guards, and with a quick sweep, knocked the men off their feet.

The rest of the guards began to charge in now, and rather than drop the halberd, Oberon snapped the head off of it, before settling into a defensive stance, facing the six men coming from the gate holding the halberd shaft as if it were a staff.

Almost pitying those men, Sordrel launched the halberd he was carrying over the wall, and turned toward the two messengers that had been about to enter the mansion. They carried swords rather than halberds, presumably so they could run faster, but the lack of reach would prove disastrous for them.

Sordrel was one of the weaker Immortals in combat, having had almost no time to train, and he found it difficult to swallow his irrational fear at facing two armed men. He knew they couldn't really harm him, but those swords looked menacing regardless. With an angry shake of his head, he went on the offense as they split apart to flank him, charging at the man on his right, and dodging away from the man's panicked thrust, grabbed him by the arm. Smashing down with his other arm, Sordrel broke the man's sword-arm with a horrendous snapping sound, before turning to face the other guard.

The other guard came on angrily, launching a vicious slash toward Sordrel's chest. Sordrel jumped back, almost tripping over the other guard, who was kneeling on the ground clutching his arm. The guard kept on, keeping Sordrel off balance and forcing him backward, until suddenly Oberon came upon him from behind, and smashed the man's hand with the halberd shaft, causing him to drop his sword with a cry of pain.

Oberon glanced at Sordrel, clearly unimpressed.

"That was sloppy, Sordrel. Pay more attention."

Sordrel nodded silently, and looked toward the place Oberon had been fighting the other guards. Their halberds were shattered upon the ground, and the men themselves were cowering in submission, seemingly uninjured.

Oberon took the swords off the ground and tossed them casually over the wall, before taking a look at the man Sordrel had injured, grabbing his arm and touching it lightly near the break.

"This is a nasty break. Sortira would have your hide if she saw this. You've shattered the bone rather than snapping it cleanly."

Sordel sighed. "We have more important things to worry about, Oberon. See to these men, I'll go see who our mystery leader is."

As Sordrel began walking toward the enormous double doors of the mansion, they opened, and a man he recognized immediately walked out of them.

Varan looked different than he remembered. The last time he had seen him the man had been wearing loose and shapeless garb, to better conceal his build, and his profession. Now the man seemed to exult in his nobility.

He stood tall, wearing a tight, embroidered tunic, which displayed both wealth and his impressive physique. He gave Sordrel a calculating look before speaking.

"If you're going to conquer my city, Sordrel, the least you could do is wear a shirt."

Sordrel glanced down for a moment, taken by surprise by Varan's new tone and demeanor.

"You're very different than I remember, Varan."

Varan shrugged haughtily. "Of course I am. Did you forget that I'm a spy? I am the person that each situation calls for, and at the moment Varngrim needs me to play noble. It would seem that my efforts to defend the city were in vain, but until your conquest is complete, this persona is necessary."

Sordrel nodded. "It doesn't suit you, or anyone, to act so arrogant."

Varan shrugged again. "I could never keep the nobles and their men in line if I couldn't convince them that I'm a suitable heir for Lord Greis, and I needed them to give Varngrim the best chance of remaining free. After seeing your friend in action, it seems that was a vain hope, however. Give me a moment to signal the surrender."

Varan gave a signal toward the house, and a stream of men exited, and began running out of the gate to deliver their messages. As they left, one of the crows flying above the city called Sordrel's attention to the north. A swarm of men with torches was now heading toward the Greis household, it appeared that the disturbance had been the beginnings of a riot. Sordrel alerted the other Immortals, but they hadn't secured the south yet, he and Oberon would need to handle the rioters on their own.

"Varan, there are rioters coming down from the

north side of the city. Do you know who they are?"

Varan cursed, and for a brief moment the guise of arrogant noble was replaced by an honest expression of disgust. "Damn the masses. With all the noble refugees buying out space in the south, all of our laborers have been forced to the north end of the city. With the food shortages, it's become a slum over the last few weeks. I had to introduce martial law when you people assassinated Greis," He gave Sordrel a dark look, "It was easy enough to keep the nobles in line by assimilating their guards into the defense of the city, but I've needed to maintain a continuous military presence up there to prevent a riot. I guess your invasion gave them the chance they needed."

Sordrel scowled at Varan. "So you've been keeping starving people under control by force? That's horrifying, Varan."

Varan scowled back. "I don't have the power to make food appear out of thin air, Sordrel. The more cities you conquer, the more refugees you create. Refugees cause shortages, and shortages cause chaos. Enough politics, I need to get the remaining guards ready to deal with the riot."

Sordrel shook his head. "We'll deal with the rioters. Get in the house, you've done enough."

Varan shrugged as he turned to return to the manor house. "Going to use your mind control? Or are you just going to allow them to slaughter the evil nobles in the hopes of sating their bloodlust?"

Sordrel simply sighed and shook his head as Varan closed the door behind himself. He and Oberon began carrying the soldiers into the house, and were soon helped by the servants. As they worked, the light from approaching torches grew continuously brighter, and they began to hear the shouting, crashes, and footsteps that heralded the approach of the mob. The mob was soon at the gate, and Sordrel addressed them from behind the gate, having to shout to be heard over the chants and yells calling for the death of the nobility. He kept his will in check, preventing it from adding its subtle manipulations to his words.

"Greetings, citizens. I am Sordrel of the Immortals, we've just secured the-"

One of the rioters interrupted him "Open the gate, tyrant! You're no Immortal!"

The rioters started slamming into the gate, and as those in the back continued pushing forward, found themselves pinned against it. The continuous pressure to move forward from the back eventually caused the gate to buckle, and the unfortunate rioters who had been in front collapsed to the ground, only be to be trampled by those behind them.

Sordrel and Oberon, at first too stunned to react to the buckling gate, rushed forward to stop the mob from trampling its own people, but even with their strength they couldn't push back the force of hundreds of people trying to force their way in. Instead of pushing back the mob, they found themselves trapped within it, being buffeted on all sides by the force of the wave of human bodies pushing itself into the courtyard. It was only their supernatural strength that allowed them to stand fast, doing their best to shield the fallen.

After what seemed an eternity, the mob stopped surging forward, and Sordrel was given a chance to look around. The courtyard was now full of men, some wielding torches, others pitchforks, hammers, or other improvised weapons from tools of labor. Those nearby caught sight of the men and women on the ground, with Sordrel and Oberon standing near them, and a cry went up through the crowd that the guards had taken down some of their number. The crowd began to surge again, this time centered inward toward the two Immortals, and they found themselves fighting men on all sides, some armed with weapons, but with no space to effectively use them.

It was a fight of brute force, Sordrel found himself punched, kicked, stabbed, and bludgeoned as he frantically fought to escape the swarm. He lashed out wildly, each blow from his powerful fists, arms, or legs taking down an attacker, but they were always replaced by another. He lost track of Oberon in the swarm, and felt as if he'd suffocate from the overpowering force propelling men and women after him one after another, each more crazed and vicious than the last.

Suddenly, it stopped. The people surrounding him all fell to the ground simultaneously, seemingly dead. The courtyard was filled with the bodies of the rioters, having fallen prone atop each other. There were only two other figures standing. Oberon, and a dark figure Sordrel instantly recognized as Comanatin.

'I expected better Sordrel. Get these people under control. Sorelin won't be able to hold Sveria for long.'

It was then that Sordrel noticed the people who had fallen were still moving slightly, their expressions were terrified, and their eyes moved, but they seemed otherwise held in place.

'Now, Sordrel.'

Sordrel's mind seemed to clear and he knew what

he needed to do. His will worked off the feelings that already existed, and diplomacy was no longer an option. These people had started off angry, and were now terrified. He would need to use that fear to get them under control, and prevent the crowd from attacking again once Comanatin left. The only sounds in the area were the disturbing crunching and cracking noises of bones moving and being set, as Comanatin began healing the wounded, even as they lay paralyzed. Knowing the unsettling background noise would only aid his attempts to instill obedience, and with the full backing of his will enhancing his presence, he spoke with the force of a spurned god.

"We came as liberators, but you have spurned us with your mindless violence. We are now conquerors. When you can again rise, you will not, until you are given orders to do so. We are in absolute control. Disobedience will be swiftly punished. This city now belongs to the Immortals. There are no nobles, no peasants, only people. Your grievances with the people of this household are at an end."

Sordrel was interrupted by a strange sensation, as if a part of him had disappeared, but he couldn't put his finger on what. Before he could think longer on it, however, Comanatin disappeared suddenly in a rush of wind. The people on the ground began moving fingers experimentally, but nobody stood up.

Sordrel nodded to Oberon. "Begin taking groups of ten back to their homes."

**

Sorelin did not like being put on a leash like this.

He and Comanatin had been corralling Sveria toward the mountains for weeks, but despite her injured and weakened state, Comanatin refused to head in for the kill, claiming she was too dangerous.

'I need to deal with something in Varngrim, Sorelin. Keep your distance so she doesn't realize I'm gone. I'll be back shortly.'

Sorelin was maintaining three separate copies of both himself and Comanatin, some nearer Sveria, and some further away, but all on her far side, amidst the swarm of shamblers they had brought from the forest. Realizing this might be his only chance to work without Comanatin's interference, Sorelin moved to join with one of his illusions, while keeping himself invisible and maintaining illusory pressure on Sveria with the fakes. If he allowed her to realize anything had changed she would undoubtedly break free of the trap before he had a chance to move in for the kill. At the moment she was running south, following the mountain bases rather than allowing herself to be pushed into the more hostile terrain in the mountains themselves. She had long ago stopped bothering to destroy the shamblers, as Comanatin kept reanimating them regardless, which would play right into Sorelin's hands now that Comanatin wasn't around to continue the practice.

Syncing himself inside an illusion was easy, and Sveria had fallen for the trick in the past. The idea was to convince the target that another illusion that was masked in invisibility, was you, and that you were an illusion. Moving quickly, he cycled himself and his illusion closer to Sveria, through the swarms of shamblers. One stab would end the fight, and Sveria would be no more. She didn't react at all as he came closer and closer.

When he was almost upon her, she spun suddenly toward him, a delighted grin on her face.

"Fool me once..."

A blade seemed to materialize in Sorelin's chest, he hadn't even seen it leave her hand. Coughing, he tried to back away, but Sveria was on him in a flash, blades in both hands. One slice, two, a thousand. The blades moved too quickly to count, creating lines of pain across his entire body as he collapsed to the ground, and soon into darkness.

**

Comanatin reappeared, mere moments after leaving. A mangled lump appeared beside him, that Sordrel realized to his horror, was the body of Sorelin.

'There's been a change of plan, Sordrel. The city needs to be evacuated. Get Varan's help. Tell him if the city isn't emptied as quickly as possible, Sveria will kill every single citizen, and use their blood to slaughter the next city, until humanity is destroyed utterly.'

Sordrel nodded, and said out loud.

"I'll handle it, Comanatin. I won't disappoint you again."

Comanatin didn't seem to hear him, and after a quick glance around the area, disappeared with the body once again. A startled shriek from within the mansion indicated his destination.

Sordrel addressed the still prone rioters. "I'll return shortly, nobody move until given instructions by an Immortal."

Nobody seemed willing to disobey. He didn't even need to use his will anymore, their fear was palpable. Sighing to himself at how wrong things had turned out, he entered the mansion to look for Varan.

**

Varan didn't trust the Immortals were being honest about the danger to the city from Sveria, but he had no doubt this would be his best chance to get as many people away from the Immortals as possible. In the days leading up to the assault on Varngrim, he had plenty of time to consider his choices should the city fall, and he had decided that the only chance for escaping from under the thumb of both the Immortals and Sveria was to take as many people as he could to Passwatch, and from there proceed to Midgar.

The purpose of Passwatch was to ensure that monsters from the plains couldn't make their way into the lands of men, and occasionally to send units to combat any monsters that came out of the mountains. Every citizen of Passwatch was a soldier, and unlike the rest of the cities, they had no nobility, only officers. Passwatch relied wholly upon the other cities for basic necessities, however. The nobles were terrified that the people of Passwatch would someday decide to forsake their appointed task, and instead use their martial might to crush the noble armies and usurp power in a bloody coup.

This fear led the noble houses in the other cities to secure complete control over the basic necessities that Passwatch needed to survive. Food, wood, metal, even manufacturing of the raw materials were done in the other cities. Passwatch citizens lived to fight. The problem with this setup was simple. The better the people of Passwatch fulfilled their duties, the less of a threat the plains seemed to the rest of humanity, and the easier it became for them to cut down on supplies to Passwatch. In the hundred years since the last major monster attack in the heartland, the population of Passwatch had halved. There simply wasn't enough food or supplies to support their old population. The periodic skirmishes with monsters that got too close to the wall that separated the lands of men from the creatures outside became more and more desperate.

Then came Midgar. Passwatch had tried several times in the past to shake off the fetters that bound it by creating satellite cities in the plains, but all had met with disaster. Midgar was different, however. It had inexplicably succeeded where others had failed, and Passwatch kept its secrets closely guarded. Through Midgar, Passwatch managed to recover from its downward spiral, and prevent a total collapse. It had created an incredibly tense situation with the rest of the cities, however, who saw an independent Passwatch as even more terrifying than the monsters they kept at bay. Before the situation with the Immortals had occurred, Varan had been certain he was going to be sent to look in on what was really going on with Midgar.

That was in the past, however. He had thought perhaps Passwatch would help combat the Immortals directly, but after having seen the power Comanatin so easily incapacitated an entire mob with, he was certain that even the soldiers of Passwatch would be helpless against him. Now his thoughts were on escape. If humanity were to escape into the plains, would the Immortals dare follow? The organization lacked leadership, and Varan suspected that they were reaching the limits of their ability to govern. If they spread their chain of command too thin by chasing refugees all the way to Midgar, they might even collapse inward. Varan hoped fleeing to Midgar would give humanity the time it needed to achieve the power necessary to fight back.

Thus, Varan had decided to help with the evacuation. He already had plans in place, and if the Immortals became distracted by the conflict with Sveria, he would be able to take advantage of the situation to escape with those who wanted to flee.

**

'You've been quiet, Comanatin. You let Sveria reach a city, didn't you?'

'Yes, Gingko, but I've got things under control. She's being flashy and wasting a lot of energy creating blood rain, telekinetic weapons, and otherwise being overly dramatic in her murder. By the time she gets here, she won't be at full strength.'

'I told you not to underestimate her, Comanatin.'

'I'll be fine. Once I revive Sorelin, I want to try something with his power.'

'His illusions don't fool her, Comanatin. He's too weak for that.'

'I don't intend to fool her. I just want to distract her for a few hours. If she continues blowing through her energy like this, it won't be long.'

'I agree, but I think we have different endings in

127

mind. I have my research to attend to, Comanatin. Stay safe.'

'I will. I'll contact you when she's back under control.'

**

As Varan looked east toward Varngrim, he found himself glad he had helped evacuate the city. He could clearly see the blood storm raging toward the city. The tempest Sveria brought from the east was one of blades, blood, and death. The downpour came not from clouds, but from a crimson lake in the sky, raining deadly, boiling blood upon the ground. The greenery shriveled and died as she passed, traveling faster than any horse could gallop. Looking upon the horror that approached, he found it hard to imagine that even a creature like Comanatin could fight against it.

Sordrel was having similar thoughts, as the pair stood watching the storm's approach in horror. After a few moments, they turned as one to get people moving again. The refugees were staring awestruck at the approaching storm, and it took everything they could to get people moving again. When they finally got them moving, however, their pace was substantially faster than before the storms appearance. Nobody wanted to be near the city anymore.

As they walked, Varan noticed that Sordrel looked worried. It was the first time he had seen the Immortal show any signs of insecurity. He was typically jovial and confident to the point of seeming arrogant. Varan decided to ask the question that had been bothering him ever since they left Varngrim.

"Are you and the rest of the Immortals going to help Comanatin?"

Sordrel looked up and shook his head sadly. "We wouldn't be any help. Comanatin says we'd just be blood sacks for her to draw energy from, and that she'd kill us all in seconds."

Varan shook his head. "Can she really be so powerful? I saw you and your friend standing firm against the mob today. The raw strength that must have taken..."

Sordrel sighed. "Nowhere near enough. You saw Comanatin. Paralyzing that entire mob, while simultaneously healing their injuries, was an offhand act for him. He's been alive since before our civilization existed, Varan. Sveria too. The power they wield..." He shuddered. "It's the reason we need Comanatin's guidance. We need power to defend ourselves, and we won't get that power on our own."

Varan wasn't convinced. "I disagree. I don't think we'll ever achieve that level of power if we allow ourselves to be shackled to a powerful benefactor."

Sordrel shrugged. "You'll see. Assuming we survive. Comanatin says he can defeat Sveria, but that lake of blood..." He shuddered again. "That's probably all that's left of the population of Bernon."

Varan eyed Sordrel carefully. "You're saying she slaughtered Bernon on her way here?"

Sordrel nodded. "That's right."

Varan's eyes widened in horror. "So much death, and for what? To choose who should reign over us as overlord? That's enough, Sordrel. Let me take these people to Midgar."

Sordrel's eyes widened. "What?"

"You think Comanatin is benevolent, but his fight with Sveria has just cost us the lives of close to ten thousand people. We just lost what, a fifth of the population of humanity? In hours, because of one slip up. We can't risk that Comanatin will lose, or that he'll turn into a tyrant. You can have this land, Sordrel. I can't save everyone, we both know you Immortals have won the war against humanity, whether you defeat Sveria or not. I can save these people though. Let me take them to Midgar, and years from now, we can argue about who was in the right."

Sordrel thought on this. Comanatin was fighting Sveria, and he would win. It was somehow inconceivable for him to lose. As he looked to those people in earshot, those who until now had been desperately trying to hide the fact that they were eavesdropping as they walked, he saw something that horrified him. Fear. These people were terrified of him. The news had spread quickly throughout the city about the events with the mob, and the tide of public opinion had shifted. These people saw the Immortals as monsters, tyrants that they were helpless to fight against. Could he convince them of their fallacy? Should he? He had no doubt that these people would be better off under Comanatin's leadership, but would they accept it? Would the fear and resentment of these people infect the rest of humanity?

Sordrel finally sighed, and shook his head sadly, defeated. "Fine, Varan. Let's turn south. We'll head for Passwatch."

As Varan was about to reply, he was interrupted by the sight of a hole appearing in the horizon. A wall of pure darkness was coming in from the southwest, heading straight for them. Things had gone from bad to worse.

**

Sveria was surprised to see Comanatin and Relin waiting for her outside the gates of Varngrim. She had expected Comanatin to flee, and Relin was dead, she had killed him, torn his body to shreds, and left it in the wilderness mere hours before. As she came closer, she could feel the vast emptiness in the city with her will. No animals, no humans, no blood. Had Comanatin's forces truly taken Varngrim in the days she fought to escape his trap?

It didn't matter. The loss of a few cities was meaningless. She had brought up humanity from nothing, and she could do it again. All that was left was to deal with Comanatin. Launching forward, she called upon the rain of boiling blood to blot out the sky above the city. As she had hoped, Comanatin teleported himself and Relin within one of manors in the city to avoid the rain. He intended to hold ground here and wait her out, the fool. With her heightened speed, she charged into the city, toward the building Comanatin had put himself in.

As she neared the building in which she felt Comanatin and Relin's presence, her world exploded in a flash of color and noise, and she momentarily reeled in shock. The sensations continued, and as she tried to deal with the overload of information, she felt a sharp stab of pain across her back, and she was hurled to the street. Her instincts snapped into action, and fighting to ignore the continuously changing lights and sounds that surrounded her, she narrowed in on the rush of air that heralded Comanatin's next destination, and slashed out with her dagger in advance.

Too late she felt the air around her explode outward, and in the fraction of a second it took for her to recover from Comanatin's feint, he appeared behind her and slammed her across the back again with what she now recognized to be a heavy staff. The illusionary cacophony was distracting, but she was already learning to focus on reality. As the force of Comanatin's blow slammed her to the ground again, she kicked backward, only for him to disappear once more.

Trying to breathe, she found herself in a vacuum. At first she couldn't feel why amidst the illusions, but after a moment she realized Comanatin had created a barrier of force to prevent the air from reaching her. It was quite a strong barrier, but with so much blood to draw upon, it took almost no effort to destroy. As the air rushed back in the illusions vanished, and she felt with her will to figure out where Comanatin had gone now. He and Relin were now in a different house, a substantial distance away.

Sveria stretched, and considered her options. Comanatin's attacks were useless against her in her current state. He simply wasn't strong enough to cause her harm. His magical powers were irritating, but not dangerous. The problem was her inability to reach him. He could teleport anywhere in the city at will. There was also his healing capability to take into account. The unpleasant thought came to her that if she decapitated him he'd reattach his head before his body had the decency to hit the ground. He was not invincible, however. His powerful will and magic were fundamentally based within his brain. If she cleaved his skull in two she was relatively sure he would die, and with her heightened abilities from the lake of blood, it just might be possible to accomplish. If not she could certainly force him to flee, and with him gone take back her nation from the traitors.

As she began running toward his new location, she felt a sudden sense of unease, the air had changed suddenly, as in the calm before a storm, and she instinctively looked to the south and west to see a dark void on the horizon, approaching rapidly. It was still too far to sense with her will, but it emitted a certain sense of wrongness even this far out, as if its very existence was influencing the wills of everything within a wide range. Gingko was coming.

Sveria launched herself toward Comanatin's location. The void on the horizon would arrive within minutes, and while her victory against Comanatin was inevitable with only the two of them, the addition of Gingko to the fight would add a level of uncertainty she was uncomfortable with. Gingko had always been more dangerous than Comanatin. While he played with his reanimated toys, she manipulated the very essence of will, and created artificial monstrosities to destroy her enemies. Sveria was loathe to think of how powerful the woman could have become over the centuries.

Comanatin seemed to recognize Gingko's approach as well, and as Sveria neared him, he teleported halfway across the city, seeming content to wait for her arrival. Relin had disappeared; Sveria supposed Comanatin wanted to hold him in reserve until he was going on the offensive again. If Comanatin teleported away now, he would be unable to return until a minion arrived to extend his will. That would hopefully give Sveria enough time to deal with Gingko. Drawing blood from the lake above her, she created swarms of blades to descend upon the city. She spread them within a wide range, and as Comanatin teleported around the city, the blades weaved a tighter and tighter web, cutting through the very buildings to reach their destinations. As she finished the web, she started on the offensive, bringing the nearby blades around to attack Comanatin as he teleported in.

To her surprise, he did not flee as she anticipated, and instead took to the sky, teleporting into the air at the halfway point between the ground and the blood lake. Scowling, Sveria drew even more blood out of the rapidly diminishing lake, and created another web, this one three dimensional, to begin covering the air space. As the web approached total coverage, however, Gingko arrived, and the city was plunged into darkness.

The darkness that covered the area was more than the simple absence of light. Sveria could sense it as a giant singular will, with two focal points that had physical form, and the rest incorporeal. Gingko herself had remained outside the range of Sveria's blades, and Comanatin remained airborne, weaving through Sveria's web unharmed, like a spider.

Sveria was for a moment at a loss for how to react. As the darkness fully settled upon the city, it began to drain the heat from the air, and the temperature was dropping rapidly. Two creatures, the physical manifestations of the dark void's will, were flying toward her quickly, and at first based on their shape, Sveria thought they were small dragons, only double or triple the size of a man. The proportions were wrong though. They had distinctive arms, unlike the quadrupedal dragons, and their wills were strange, seeming to mesh with the surrounding darkness, as if they weren't independent creatures at all, merely the physical appendages of an otherwise incorporeal creature.

As the creatures entered the city, Sveria set her blades on them immediately, but they had no apparent vital organs, no weak points, and the deep cuts into their flesh seemed to not slow them in the least. Any wounds they sustained simply vanished instantly and her telekinetic blades didn't have enough force to cleave through their powerful frames and dismember them. Deciding to ignore them, she launched herself toward Gingko as the temperature continued to drop around her.

As her array of blades approached Gingko, the necromancer flew almost casually into the air, and began dodging around the projectiles as the field of cold surrounding Sveria grew even colder. Sveria herself closed the distance quickly, and flung herself into the air after Gingko. She could feel the blood pool above her diminishing rapidly, but she dared not remove the blade array until she had brought the odds in her favor again by killing one of the necromancers.

Sveria hadn't flown in decades, preferring the feel of the ground under her feet, and it showed in her pursuit. Gingko managed to evade her for many precious seconds before Sveria's blood fueled speed finally allowed her to corner her within her blade network. As she plunged her daggers toward Gingko, however, the necromancer vanished in a rush of wind, only to appear between her minions, some distance away.

Sveria snarled in rage. Things were going poorly.

These necromancers were too slippery to land a hit on, and she was running out of blood to fuel her abilities. She cursed herself for allowing herself to become so weak, and, dismissing the wall of blades, began her retreat to the south.

**

'Where are you going, Sordrel?'

'You were busy and a decision had to be made. I'm escorting the refugees to Passwatch. From there, those who wish to join us can, and those who want to go to Midgar can.'

There was a pause. 'You've stumbled right into Sveria's path. You can't move laterally, you won't get out of her path by the time she crosses yours. Continue due south toward Passwatch and get those people moving as fast as possible. Your lives depend on Sveria being incapacitated before she overtakes you. After seeing Sorelin, she won't make the mistake of leaving the head intact again.'

Sordrel was visibly shaken, and Varan noticed. "What is it? Did Comanatin die?"

Sordrel shook his head, and simply said "She's coming."

**

Comanatin had been only mildly surprised when Gingko showed up. Sveria was an incredible specimen, and a chance to get first hand information about her capabilities was not one to pass up lightly, despite the danger. Despite his warning to Sordrel, he was confident the situation was under control now.

Despite their years apart, Comanatin and Gingko still fought in perfect tandem. Wraith and Shade served to distract Sveria, as their powerful swings could rend her limb from limb if she allowed them to get in a solid hit, while Gingko herself gave form to the living darkness that surrounded Sveria, landing blow after blow with masses of the living darkness, given physical form for mere moments to launch crushing attacks.

Comanatin had ensured that Sveria's path remained barred with walls of shamblers. Every turn Sveria had to make to bypass a wall of flesh without slowing prevented her from making progress in her desired direction. She had run out of external blood minutes ago, and had been under continuous assault ever since. Comanatin continued teleporting shamblers from the north into the fight, hoping to finally overwhelm the powerful warrior, and force her surrender.

Still she fought, however, and showed no signs of tiring, dodging every attack launched by Wraith or Shade, and even some of Gingko's attacks with the darkness itself. The shamblers she mostly ignored, their feeble attacks did nothing to harm the powerful woman, but their presence slowed her and reduced her options for retreat or evasion. She had learned by now that any damage she caused to the minions was simply healed, and she only cut where necessary to clear a path to Gingko, who she seemed to consider the larger threat.

Comanatin was surprised by her insistence on continuing the fight. She had already been beaten at this point, it was simply a matter of time before she was overwhelmed by attacks she had no counter for. Her fierceness was amazing, and cornered as she was, she fought almost as well as she had previously when fueled with the blood. Comanatin wondered whether the blood was truly necessary, or if it was simply some twisted fetish of hers that honed her abilities via psychosoma.

In either case, it was time for this to end. With a silent signal to Gingko, Comanatin teleported himself into the fray as well, grabbing at Sveria's arms from behind as masses of dark tendrils did the same. He immediately kicked down at the back of her knee as more tendrils came to pull her forward. Put off balance by the sudden combination of attacks, Sveria collapsed to the ground, bound within the darkness.

At first she struggled, but as it became clear that there would be no escape, she simply scowled at Comanatin.

"So this is it then? You intend to enslave me like your other pets? I think you'll find my will to be far too strong to dominate."

Gingko spoke aloud, likely for the first time in centuries. "You are my captive, Sveria, and I have no interest in your mind. That is Comanatin's field. You're clearly too dangerous to study in captivity, but perhaps in the wild, far from here? Your love of elves is quite apparent in your manner toward my friend, and thus I think it is time you got to know them better."

The ball of darkness in which Sveria was bound began to ascend, with Wraith and Shade following. As the ball rose, Gingko waved a farewell to the bound warrior, "Have fun in the jungle, Sveria. I'll be keeping an eye on you, don't disappoint me by dying."

With that, the ball of darkness sped into the distance, carrying Sveria far to the south and out of sight.

'Thank you for your help, Gingko.'

'I told you so, old friend.'

'Indeed. Will you be staying awhile or returning to your isolation?'

'I have work to get back to, Comanatin. Imbued pyromancy won't invent itself, and your mortal playthings will need their puppet master.'

'Very true. I hope witnessing Sveria in action for yourself gave you some ideas. I certainly have some experiments that need running because of the events today.'

'Oh yes. I'll also be keeping a mote of will near her until she manages to destroy it. I'll share any data I glean from that with you.'

'Excellent. Farewell Gingko, and thank you again for your timely assistance.'

'Anytime, old friend.'

**

The journey to Passwatch was going more smoothly than Varan had anticipated. He had feared that once Comanatin was done with Sveria, he would come upon them in a fury at Sordrel's treachery. That had no happened, however. Varan immediately noticed when Comanatin contacted Sordrel, by the way the huge man had stiffened, but that conversation apparently went well, as after his initial tension, he quickly settled into his more cheerful demeanor, which had been hidden beneath the stress of the last few weeks. After a few minutes of speaking mentally with his master, his smile growing broader by the second, he finally turned to Varan.

"The war is over, Varan. Passwatch won't involve itself in an internal conflict, Sveria is going on a very long trip, and Comanatin has given the go ahead for you to take as many refugees to Midgar as necessary. We won't hold anyone here against their will."

Varan nodded, finding himself once again in the uncomfortable position of speaking for humanity. "I'm glad to hear that. Perhaps there's hope for those who stay behind after all."

Sordrel grinned. "You're welcome to stay, Varan. We have no interest in forcing people from their homes and livelihoods, though I think you'll find less need for spies with the nobility gone. Perhaps you could write something interesting for a change."

Varan shook his head. "I can't, Sordrel. I understand that you trust this necromancer, but I don't have that luxury, and neither do most of the people here. You seem like a good man, Sordrel, and I'm trusting that you'll do what you can to protect the people that stay, but I don't trust Comanatin, and I don't trust the nest of serpents we're escorting either."

He glanced toward the procession of nobles, who kept themselves apart from the rest of the refugees. "These people hold grudges, Sordrel, and I need to make sure those grudges don't undermine our position in Midgar. If Midgar falls, we can only rely on the benevolence of the necromancer, and I have to do everything in my power to prevent that."

Sordrel nodded. "I understand. I'll do my best here, and you do what you can there. Maybe one day, there won't be the need for separation any longer, and we can bring humanity back together."

**

Once Passwatch was in sight, the refugees came to a halt, and set up an encampment. There was no way they were going to fit an entire city's worth of people into the military base. Rather than set up camp with a bunch of peasants, the nobles immediately went on to the military base with Varan and Sordrel following close behind at a more leisurely pace.

As Sordrel and Varan arrived, they found the nobles unsurprisingly involved in a heated argument about who had the authority to speak to the Captain, they had splintered into factions on the trip here, and they apparently had never reached a resolution. The guard was very quickly losing patience, when Sordrel shouted from behind.

"Shut up, all of you!"

The command reeled through the nobles, who momentarily lapsed into terrified silence. The captain at the gate raised an eyebrow to Sordrel. "And you are?"

The nobles all immediately began shouting again, "He's the monster!"

"Arrest him!"

"Kill him!"

Sordrel sighed, and brought his will to bear, his voice carrying over the shouting nobles without seeming to be raised. "I am Sordrel, leader of the Immortals. These idiots are prisoners of war that I've been far too lax with," he gave them a scowl, and the implied threat quieted them down again. "I would speak with whoever is in charge here, Captain. We have much to discuss."

The captain looked at the cowering nobles, and then back to the shirtless behemoth of a man that stood before him. Shaking his head silently at how his day had gone from strange to downright bizarre, he gave the order and had Sordrel brought, under heavy guard, to see the commander.

The commander did not look pleased to see Sordrel. "Why have you brought an army of refugees to my doorstep, and why aren't you wearing a shirt?"

Sordrel looked down and sighed. "These refugees are going to need to make a choice. Some are going to need to be brought to Midgar, and the rest will be going home, as for the shirt, it's too damn hot out, I don't see how people outside the forest wear so much in direct sunlight."

The commander laughed derisively. "You think Midgar is a vacation destination, do you? Only Passwatch citizens are allowed in Midgar, if you northerners think you can waltz right in and screw up the first successful colony we've ever had, you have another thing coming."

Sordrel shook his head. "I'm not asking, sir. I am the leader of the Immortals, we control the north now, not the nobles, and we will be responsible for security now, not you. You have done a wonderful thing for humanity but-"

The commander interrupted. "You idiot northerners are all the same, you think you can come in here and dismantle centuries of security with a word?"

Sordrel's look stopped the commander in his tracks. "I am no ignorant noble playing childish power games. I am the leader of the Immortals, and my best soldier could take out your entire camp here." The commander bristled, "That isn't a threat, it's just a fact, and you know damn well it's possible, because you've been to Midgar and your new friends could do the same."

The commander's look of anger immediately turned to one of shock, before he resolved himself back to anger. "I don't know what you think you know about Midgar, but clearly you're dangerous. I'm placing you under arrest."

Sordrel shook his head. "That is not possible, sir. We are in control here, not you."

Sortira and Oberon suddenly appeared behind Sordrel, near the doorway.

Sordrel didn't even spare them a glance, and his voice took on a steely tone. "My word is law. Your services are no longer needed here commander, we can do this either the easy way or the hard way. The refugees who no longer wish to remain will go to Midgar, or they will die on the plains. It is up to you and your soldiers to ensure that the better of those two options occurs. I would love to offer you and your men the chance to stay, but the safety of these people comes first, and part of the surrender agreement requires that the Immortals not step foot beyond Passwatch. Humanity is splitting, commander, and it'll be up to you to ensure the security of those who are in Midgar."

The commander was stunned, the sudden appearance of the extra soldiers was clearly supernatural, which meant the rest of humanity apparently had will users now, and they were far more advanced than anyone here in Passwatch. The strongest soldiers were all in Midgar defending it against constant attacks. He sighed.

"I'm listening, Immortal, what do you want?"

**

The discussions went on for hours, but eventually the commander relented, and humanity split, just as Varan and Sordrel had desired. Thousands of the refugees decided to go on to Midgar, and as they were about to leave the outpost, they were joined by the missing nobles, who appeared in a sudden rush of wind. The soldiers of Passwatch led them to Midgar, and due to the heroics of many, not the least being Varan himself, most of the refugees made it all the way to the city. The refugees would eventually put down the roots that would turn Midgar from the small plains colony it was, into the empire it is today.

Varan came to be quite well respected on the journey, and was eventually heralded as a hero for saving those he could from the necromancer's forces. It is in the university he eventually founded that I now write this history.

When the gates closed behind the refugees, it was the end of an era. A swarm of the walking dead silently appeared to begin their eternal vigil, and the gates have remained closed ever since. It is here that the War of the Dead comes to an end, and the Rise of Midgar begins.

It is not for me to say what happened to those who remained behind the wall at Passwatch, nor shall I pass judgment of right and wrong. I would encourage every resident of Midgar, however, to think deeply upon what another war with the Immortals would mean, before the frenzy that has overtaken the city in recent years consumes us all.

ABOUT THE AUTHOR

Most know Latilya, not by name, but merely as "That weird girl in the library who's always laughing while reading the history books."

Latilya's Books can be found in print at www.createspace.com and as e-books at www.smashwords.com/profile/view/Latilya or on Amazon's Kindle.

Made in the USA
Charleston, SC
10 October 2012